Take a Knee

CHERYL BARTON

Published by: Cheryl Barton Publishing, LLC

For permission requests, write to the publisher, addressed "Attention: Permissions Coordinator," at the address below.

Cheryl Barton Publishing, LLC
P.O. Box 962
Reisterstown, Maryland 21136
www.crbarton.com

Ordering Information:
Quantity sales. Special discounts are available on quantity purchases by corporations, associations, and others. For details, contact the publisher at the address above.

Orders by U.S. trade bookstores and wholesalers. Please contact prez@crbarton.com

ISBN: 1948950014
ISBN-13: 978-1-948950-01-5

1 – Take a Knee

Kenrick Wilson walked across the massive football field after one of the best games he'd ever played as the number one quarterback in the professional league. His cleats crunched on the lightly snow covered green artificial turf field made of artificial grass with ground up recycled rubber tires. He smiled as the fans who sat in over eighty-two thousand seats in the New Jersey stadium screamed his name and waved in solidarity with the team, congratulating them on their winning streak.

"Way to go Kenrick!" one fan shouted.

"Great job, QB," another hollered.

"We support you, QB!" a few more screamed.

Kenrick smiled even brighter as he made his way through the tunnel to the team locker room where he would spend the next hour being interviewed by the media as he counted down the hours when he could return to Alpine, New Jersey to spend the next week with his family before he was off again to the next city for his next game. He loved playing for the number one professional New York football team in the league, but still couldn't get use to the fact that there was no stadium in New York, so they had to share a stadium in New Jersey. Either way, there were no greater fans than those that lived in New York or New Jersey and he loved bringing them the win.

As soon as he entered the locker room, he joined in the team celebration as the coaches spread accolades around the room. He had to admit, they played a great game which turned out to be a shutout of thirty-eight to zero. The team had found their niche and were in sync the minute they took to the field which accounted for one win after another.

"Here's our QB," head coach Mason said as he patted him on the back. "Get changed quick, Kenrick. The press is waiting to hear from you."

Kenrick nodded without responding as he headed for the shower to change. He hoped the questions would be limited in number at least for today. Now that the game was over, his mind was focused on the love of is live, Justine Banks and their three children, Erick, Ricky and their new baby, Jazmine, who he aptly calls Jazzy. The name was of course a nickname, but also because even at four months old, she had already developed a diva personality that was all her own. She had him wrapped around her cute little fingers and even her brothers at age four and six catered to her every whimper and cry.

He hopped in the shower, washed quickly and hopped out just as fast. He would take a longer shower when he got home to the safety of Justine's arms. Everyone who knew him knew that his priority after a game was getting home to his family. Usually they were at his games, but Justine wasn't ready to bring Jazmine around the crowds of people yet.

Throwing on a team t-shirt and a pair of jeans, he headed in the room where the press waited for him. As he walked through the door, someone slapped a team hat on his head, something he forgot in his rush. Taking his seat behind the microphone, the questions started immediately and he knew the first one would be about what the team did the moment they reached the field and not about the best game they'd ever played.

He'd been with the team for eight years after being selected as the number one draft pick fresh out of college by his home team. Nothing made him prouder than to play for New York, not far from New Jersey where he had been born and raised, though in a much less affluent part than where he currently lived. What he didn't want to do was think of his tumultuous past because no doubt, it would show on his face during the interview. Instead, he kept his mind on his family and the incredible game.

Before he or anyone else could make a statement to control the press conference, questions were thrown at him from all directions and not one was about the actual game, frustrating him. He still kept a smile plastered on his face.

"So, Kenrick, about tonight's sign of protest, we saw you lead your team in taking a knee. Unlike a lot of other fans in other cities, the fans here support you and the team like none we've seen so far. Do you think taking a knee will start the conversation?" one reporter asked.

Kenrick looked over at his coach who was about to interject, but he stopped him. The coach knew that he didn't plan to continue to address why he supported the effort of other sports teams across the country, professional and college level. Today, he would answer their questions and hopefully they could move on and actually talk about the football game.

"If the conversations address the actual issues, I'm fine with it. Too many people think we're a bunch of high paid athletes who shouldn't have a complaint or an issue as if money heals all wounds, but it doesn't. There are people who are being persecuted by those who don't have a right to do so and my team and I are merely using our platform as a way to say we support a change in how everyday citizens are treated. We believe all lives matter and it's time respect for all life takes precedence. If a conversation starts, then our support is well worth it," Kenrick commented.

"So, you're not bothered by how the focus of each game is being placed on the protest or the taking of the knee and not on the game?"

Kenrick looked around the crowded room, packed from wall to wall with reporters with note pads and cameras videotaping and flashing in his face. He wasn't sure who asked the question, but he knew everyone wanted to ask it. He responded to the crowd in general.

"Were you at the game? Today was to be all about the game and that was it. We're not distracted, we're focused. The fans aren't distracted, they're focused. Taking of the knee took a few seconds, but like I mentioned, if it starts a conversation, then good. We're not being disrespectful and we're not hurting anyone. We have the utmost respect for the flag and for the national anthem, but what those two things stand for, should represent everyone in this country, not some. Now, if anyone has a question about the game, let's have it because I have a family to get home to," he noted.

Everyone laughed and the mood was immediately lightened.

"Okay, let me start by saying congratulations on the new addition to your family recently. We're used to seeing your family in the stands and your boys are missed at the table with you today. They are the highlight of every interview we do with you following your games. How are Justine and the baby doing?" a reporter asked.

Just the mentioning of Justine's name got an even brighter smile out of him.

"The family is great and Justine and Jazmine are doing really good. She's anxious to get back in the stands to support me."

Kenrick signaled for the next reporter to ask a

question, one he knew would stay on task.

"Kenrick, you played the game of your life today. How does it feel to shut the other team completely out?"

"The entire team was on fire today. We are a well-oiled machine and have worked hard for this kind of winning streak. I celebrate this win with them because it was a team effort," he explained.

Kenrick answered one question after the other and tried to keep his answers short. The minute one of the guys asked about his family, that was all he could think about.

He loved looking out in the stands and seeing Justine, their kids and his brother Josiah and his family in the stands, sporting his jersey and cheering him on to success. His family wasn't as large as others, but they brought their support as if they were a crowd of hundreds. For the next several weeks, he would be away from them for a few away games and wanted as much time with them as he could get. He'd waited what seemed a lifetime to have his own family and now that he had one, he wanted his free time spent with them, showing them love around the clock, something he didn't receive as a child.

When questions turned to other players who shared the stage with him, he looked to his coach who signaled he was ending the interviews soon. Coach Mason was one of the few people who knew what being with his family meant to him and knew how eager he was to get on the road to get home.

After another ten minutes of questions, Coach Mason finally ended the interview.

"Okay, the players gave you an outstanding game today and they would like to get out of here and unwind. You can submit other questions and we'll get you responses in print."

Kenrick didn't wait for the end of his coach's speech. He moved away from the table and slipped out of the side door to head back to the locker room to grab his gear. He wanted to make the best of his next few days off. After putting in a quick text message to his security team to meet him at the players entrance, he once again congratulated his fellow players and headed out.

When he reached the car with the head of his security, Cesar, driving, he didn't have to tell him where he wanted to go. He'd spent the last two nights in a hotel in Jersey along with the other players, something the coach required they do to avoid any distractions. Now released, Justine and his munchkins were all he wanted. After getting into the back of the shiny black Navigator truck and Cesar drove off towards his home, he pulled out his phone and called Justine.

"Hey there, sweetness," he raved the minute she answered.

"Hey, babe! Good game today! You rocked. How are you feeling?" she said.

Kenrick loved the sound of her voice. Anytime he was having a bad day, hearing it made him smile.

"Fantastic now that I'm on my way home. I wasn't

sure how much of the game you were able to catch."

"I caught all of it. The boys were glued to the television and thankfully your feisty daughter slept through most of it. I even put them all in their jerseys as they watched you play. Ricky said he saw you wave when the camera was on you. I can't wait to see you."

He was glad his son caught their signal. Whenever they weren't at the game, he told them he would always wave to them during the game to let them know he was thinking about them. He wasn't sure Erick would catch it, but he knew it wouldn't get by Ricky. He was a sport fanatic like his father and never took his eyes off of any plays.

"Ditto, baby. You know how I am after a game, I need you," he expressed.

"I'll be here when you get here and the kids will all be asleep. Jazzy is a loose cannon though. She's hit or miss when it comes to sleeping or wanting to wake up and play," Justine quipped.

"Our daughter is a little blocker! I'll talk to her when I get home. She loves the sound of her daddy's voice and I'll promise her a rose garden if she lets us have a quiet night without interruption. I can be persuasive when needed and tonight there is a need."

"I've missed you," Justine admitted.

Music to his ears and he felt like that twenty-one year old he was when he first met her years ago. Even back then, Justine's voice had a smoky, sultry sound to it that made him want her more and more. She still had that impact on him.

"I've missed you, too. How did the boys do watching it on television after you told them they couldn't come to my game? I know they knew I played in town tonight."

Kenrick knew that his youngest didn't care, but Ricky loved being in the stadium. Not only did they attend his home games, but Justine often flew to his away games and brought the boys with her. Things changed with Jazmine being born. Soon, things would get back to normal and the baby would become one of many at the stadium.

"They were fine. I explained to them that because their uncle was out of town and their grandpa wasn't coming in this week for the game, they couldn't go because I couldn't take Jazzy with how cold is. I wasn't ready to leave her at home with the nanny yet," Justine explained.

"Good. I don't want my baby girl left with anyone yet."

"You know Hannah is good with her and I leave Jazmine with her when I need to do a quick run. You are going to spoil her," Justine said.

Kenrick liked the nanny Justine picked for the boys and she was good with Jazmine, but he felt that Jazmine was still too young to be left with anyone for hours at a time.

"She's spoiling me. Every time I hold her in my arms and look into her pretty little face, I can't help but want to protect her from everything and love her more than life itself," he said.

"No worries because the minute anyone has to deal with your daughter's crying, they'll be running to give her back to us," Justine laughed.

Kenrick chuckled along with her.

"I have something special planned for you, tonight," he whispered. He knew his driver wasn't paying attention, but Rod, the other guy on his security detail who rode in the back of the truck with him could hear every word even if he tried to act like he couldn't hear.

"Really? Am I going to love it?" Justine asked.

"Don't you always? I know I will."

"Down, boy!" Justine jibed. "Remember, this is how we got Jazzy. Your pull-out game isn't what it should be and Jazzy should have a few years of being the youngest before another one pops out," she added.

Kenrick doubled over in laughter. He was glad the occupants of the truck couldn't hear her response.

"I hear you and I've noted that. What did the doctor say about taking Jazzy on a plane for my next game? We're playing in Florida and if you're coming, I want to make sure arrangements are made at your favorite hotel."

When Jazmine was born, they agreed to wait until she was at least four months old before having them travel to a game.

"She said Jazzy is good to go and I'm glad it's a weekend game. Ricky would be angry if he had to miss the game because of school during the week. We'll be there. Now, hurry and get home. I'm giving them dinner, they'll get baths and in bed by the time you get here. I love you," Justine said.

"I love you more, baby. See you in a few," Kenrick declared and hung up. "Step on it, Cesar. My baby is waiting on me," he laughed.

"No one would believe me if I told them how mushy the one hundred million man got every time he heard his woman's voice," Cesar joked.

"No one had better ever hear about it either. When you meet a woman like her, you'll understand," Kenrick joked as Cesar sped through traffic. Even Rod who seldom showed emotion laughed.

2 – Take a Knee

Justine turned left and then right as she glanced at herself in the floor to ceiling mirror at her favorite lingerie store in New York City. Even though it was a brisk, cold November day, the inside of the store was warm and toasty where women could try on sexy nighties as she was doing. At age thirty and now that she was getting her body back in shape after having her third child, she was looking forward to getting back in her sexy, nightly lingerie, something she knew the love of her life, Kenrick loved seeing her in. She loved him even more when he told her that her body was perfect for him every day. She turned left and right again and loved what she saw, loving that her time spent in their home gym was paying off.

"Justine Banks, girl, I can't believe you had a baby four months ago. You already have a flat stomach. How do you do it after each baby? I love that gold nightie.

Besides the fact that it's sexy, it's a nice combination with the gold streaks in your long hair."

Justine smiled at her best friend, Lane, as they shopped together. She and Lane had been friends since their college days at New York University in the city.

"Well, besides working out in the gym and running around behind two spry little boys, Kenrick gives me a pretty good workout," she snickered.

Lane sucked her teeth. "Oh, that's more information than I need to know, but you do look great. Kenrick is having a great season. They are going to take it all the way, you know that right and I'm going to assume that will mean a huge party at the end of the season," Lane shrieked.

"Excited much?" Justine joked. "Of course, there will be a party. We have one win or lose, so get ready. Are you planning to come for Thanksgiving dinner this year?" Justine asked.

Lane selected a few sexy pieces from the rack to try on herself, holding them up to herself before heading into the dressing room parlor.

"I wasn't sure you were having it this year with the new baby and everything," Lane said walking past her to the vacant dressing room.

Justine checked the little gold silk and lace two-piece nightie off on her list of purchases. She picked up a few more, including a long black satin gown that accentuated all of her curves. She followed Lane into the parlor and entered her dressing room.

"I wasn't sure if Kenrick wanted to or not, but he

said yes. He loves having family and friends around. My parents are coming in next week a few days before Thanksgiving. I wanted to have it catered this year, but my mom and aunt insist on cooking everything."

"Oh, then I'm definitely coming. Your mom is a beast in the kitchen with all of that southern cooking," Lane said.

"That she is and they're excited to spend more time with the kids, especially the baby. They were here when she was born for the first week, but then they had to return to Dallas. Kenrick had a game there a few weeks ago, but I wasn't ready to fly with Jazmine yet, so we stayed home. Now that she's five months old, we flew to Florida for his last game and had a good time. Kenrick has a game that Sunday before, but not on Thanksgiving Day. I'm glad because that means he'll be home and we'll all be together."

"You know, I'm happy to see you so in love. I remember back when we were in college after you'd just met him and the rocky road you went through in your relationship. All I want to know is when is the wedding? Three babies and no ring? What's going on with that?" Lane asked.

Justine felt her skin crawl the moment the words left Lane's mouth and landed on her ears. Why was everyone interested in when she and Kenrick would get married. She and her mother had the exact same conversation before she went into labor with Jazmine. In her opinion, they would get married when Kenrick was ready and he wasn't there yet.

"Don't you start, too," Justine said in response.

"What? Who else is pestering you about getting married?"

"My mom and I'm sure my dad, too, but he hasn't said anything to me about it. I have a feeling he put my mother up to asking me about it."

Out of respect when her mother asked her about them getting married, she brushed it off instead of being disrespectful by asking her to mind her business. She had been thinking it, but would never say it out loud. She was tired of being asked about it.

"Has anyone said anything to Kenrick? It's been nine years together and three kids. I know he's busy playing ball, but what's the holdup? I take it everything is still great between you two and we are out buying even more sexy lingerie as if you really need more. You know I love to shop and our trips here a few times a year are what I live for. Omar loves seeing me in this sexy, slinky stuff!" Lane declared.

Justine knew that Omar, Lane's husband and Kenrick were on the same page when it comes to what they liked to see their women in.

"Kenrick loves it too and that's why I keep it stacked up at home. I don't know why because he never leaves it on me for long and yes, everything is good between us. It gets better with each passing year. I don't know when we're getting married. That's on him. I have no doubt he knows I'll be ready whenever that is, but he's not ready yet and until he is, I don't rock the boat. I love our life and the path we took to get here is our path," Justine explained.

"Are you saying you don't care if you get married or not?" Lane asked.

"Of course, I care and I love Kenrick more than anything. I won't pressure him into getting married. He has to want to do it himself. I can tell there is something that holds him back from me fully, but I can't figure out what it is. Do you know I still don't know why he doesn't have any family to speak of?"

"Wait, I thought Paul and Minnie were his parents and Andrea was his sister."

"No, he ended up living with them when he was about fifteen and since then, he and Andrea have been brother and sister. The circumstances still aren't that clear, but I take it he had a rough childhood, something he never wants to talk about. Paul and Minnie love him like a son, but they aren't blood related. I think whatever happened to him was painful and that part of him has always been cut off from me."

Justine sat down on the bench in the dressing room after losing her desire to try on any more lingerie. Whenever she brought up Kenrick's childhood with him, he shuts down and shuts her out. She learned through trial and error to stop bringing it up.

"Is Josiah his real brother?" Lane asked.

"Yes. They found each other a few years ago. They have the same father, but different mothers. The only thing I know about his father is that he died three years ago and a week before his death the first time Kenrick ever mentioned him. He took one day to go visit his father who was in hospice dying from cancer and when he came home, he barely said anything for a week. He walked around our house like a zombie, dismissing any talk of what happened. I was fine with him doing that until it started to impact Ricky. He was confused about the lack of attention Kenrick gave him. That was the only time we've ever really argued and I told him I didn't care what was going on in his life, he is never to treat our children like castaways. He apologized profusely, not realizing he had done that. He still didn't tell me what was going on with never mentioning that his father was alive. He knew about Josiah, but didn't know where he was. He hired a private detective to find him when he began to long for his own family. Before his father died, he told him and Josiah that they had other siblings and since then, they have been on a mission to find them."

"Wow. That's a lot to take in. You think whatever happened in his childhood prevents him from committing to you fully? You're practically husband and wife, just not with the official papers."

Justine huffed in frustration, tired of answering questions about marriage. She loved Lane like a sister, but she was already tired of the conversation. She exhaled before responding so that her annoyance didn't come through.

"Kenrick is committed to me, just not to the idea of marriage right now and that's fine. I can't say what the future will hold, but our family makeup is fine and whenever Kenrick proposes, everyone who is close to me will know about it," she said and hoped that was the end of the subject.

Lane exited the dressing room and checked herself in the three-way mirror in the all-white sexy gown that she'd picked out.

"That sounds to me like your way of saying the topic is over. We've known each other too long for you to fake interest in a subject. I get it," Lane said and smiled when Justine exited the dressing room with a look that said she was sorry on her face.

"I'm not being curt about it, but everyone else is more concerned about my getting married than I am. I'm simply trying to have a happy, loving life, marriage or not."

"I hear that. When the time is right, I look forward to standing beside you on your day as you did the day I married Omar," Lane said.

When Lane reached over to hug her, the gesture almost made her cry. Justine knew everyone meant well when they asked, but it was her life and she wanted to live it her way.

"That's a bet. Now, let's get out of here because I need to get some new things for Jazzy including a snow suit now that I'm okay with her being out of the house in this cold weather. She was fine when we flew to Florida recently, but this weather we're having warrants for something much warmer than Florida attire. I also see some boot shopping in my future," Justine chimed with delight.

"Yes, boots are definitely on the menu."

Deciding to get everything she tried on, Justine grabbed her purchases from the dressing room and headed toward the cashier.

"I'll meet you out front," she shouted back to Lane.

As she reached the front of the store, she waited in line behind a woman who was telling the story of how her boyfriend had proposed to her the night before and she was showing off her ring. Justine felt a bit of jealousy while also being happy for her. All that talk about Kenrick and getting married played with her mind. Tossing it off, she perked up, congratulated the woman and put any worries she had to the side. When the time was right for her and Kenrick, it would happen.

3 – Take a Knee

Kenrick woke on Thanksgiving morning to the sound of family moving about and the smell of some of the best southern food he's ever tasted. He loved when Justine's family came for a visit because the women loved being in the kitchen cooking up all the greatest, tastiest meals.

The morning was still pretty early and he'd just flown in the day before after an away game earlier in the week where his team won again. Turning over, he smiled when he encountered the soft curves of the love of his life next to him. Nothing felt right when he was away until he came home to her and their kids. Leaning over, he kissed her neck and then her shoulders before feeling her squirm around under him.

"What time is it?" Justine stuttered out.

"It's early and your mom and aunts are already in the kitchen cooking. I love this time of year," Kenrick said.

Justine moaned and tried to move out of his embrace after feeling what he was in the mood for. She knew it had only been a few hours since she'd gotten back to sleep after getting up to feed their daughter in the middle of the night. She couldn't wait until Jazmine learned to sleep through the night. She could have let their nanny, Hannah, get up with her, but Justine loved the bonding time she had with her precious daughter.

"You do realize I've only been back to sleep a few hours. Are the boys up yet?" she asked, turning over to face him.

"Yes. Your mom got them dressed and took them down to watch cartoons until she fixed them breakfast. I could hear them talking in the hallway. I decided to not get up yet and distract the boys," he admitted.

"Did she send the entire kitchen staff home for the week?" Justine asked.

"She did. I gave them all bonuses of triple their weekly salary and they scurried off before your mother changed her mind. With your family here this week, it's good to give the staff the week off. Now, what about this extra time we have alone this morning before we have to venture out of this bedroom?" Kenrick asked, sliding over even closer to her. He knew if she continued to move away from him, she could only go so far before she ended up on the floor.

Justine opened one eye and looked into Kenrick's handsome face.

"If it's morning, why is it so dark in here?" she

asked.

"I closed all of the curtains and the panels over the skylights in the ceiling. I know you needed extra time to sleep and I wanted the room as dark as possible. Today will be a busy day with more of your family coming in later."

"Are Josiah and his family and Paul and Minnie coming?" she asked.

"They'll be here. They're the only family I have and it will be good to have them all here. Andrea is visiting for Christmas, so she won't be here for Thanksgiving."

Justine reached over and caressed his face. Even in the dark, she knew he was feeling a little sorry for himself.

"Baby, you know my family is your family, too. That's not the only family you have. There are times when I think my mother loves you more than she loves me," Justine chuckled.

Kenrick moved in close again.

"Well, right now, I love her daughter more than I love anyone and I'd like to show her how much before our kids start banging on the bedroom door begging to be let in," he said.

Kenrick captured her lips and before long, the kiss deepened as passion filled space around them.

"You do know we have family one floor away and one of us can get a little loud," Justine snickered as Kenrick reached under the black comforter that covered their king-sized bed, searching for the hem of her night shirt. Though she enjoyed the soft, warmness of the flimsy gown, she preferred her sexy nighties or sleeping in nothing at all. She had to relent while her family was in the house and put on night clothes that were more family safe.

"I'll keep it down this one time only if you let me in," Kenrick said lifting the gown from her body, tossing it to the floor and sliding her to a position under him. "You know how I get when I need to feel you," he added.

Justine moaned when she felt his hardness press against her. Her legs instinctively opened for Kenrick as he slid between her legs.

"You're already naked," she whispered against his lips when she caressed his back and then down to his behind.

"That's because I knew what I wanted the moment I opened my eyes. You know I can't be in bed with you and not want you."

Even in the darkness of their bedroom, Justine could see Kenrick's lustful gaze with his vividly dark eyes surrounded by pure white. She gasped the moment she felt him harden as his body moved around on top of hers. Needing more of him, she locked her lips with his and became enthralled at the rough, yet softness of his lips against hers. Her focus zeroed in on the feeling of him knowing she was about to get the ultimate pleasure.

"I love you," she said against his lips before Kenrick moved his lips further down her body to suckle on her breasts as an electric feeling zinged through her entire body from the contact. She loved the way he loved her.

Her hips began to move as she delighted in the feel of him hard and throbbing between her thighs. Reaching between them, she stroked his hardness from root to tip and the moment he leaned up and groaned in her ear, she knew he was already close.

"I love you more, baby. Always and forever," Kenrick said as he allowed her to guide him into her body which was already slick for his entry.

Once seated inside of her body, Justine wrapped her legs tightly around his taut waist and joined him in a rhythm that would take her to ecstasy. As he began to move quickly with hard, frenzied thrusts, she held on to his shoulders as pleasure fused throughout her body. She panted, he groaned and before long, she gripped his buttocks and bucked wildly under him as her orgasm roared through her again and again.

Kenrick could feel the evidence that he was close to his release in his uncontrollable fierce movements in and out of Justine's body. He loved that he was able to bring her to an explosive release and was now following her over that edge into an explosive vortex where only they resided.

To drown out the animalistic growl that threatened to escape, Kenrick snuggled his head between her head and shoulders and let out his groan into the pillow right next to her ear. Higher and higher his body and mind climbed as his released zipped through him as the love he had only for her took him to a new plateau. Thrusting into her body caused his climax to draw out and go on and on until finally the waves crashing through him settled and his body calmed.

It took a few moments before either of them spoke, taking in the moment. Kenrick never knew he could love anyone as much as he loved Justine and never, not even for a day, has he ever regretted anything about their love.

"This is why I love when you're home," Justine said, placing soft open mouth kisses on Kenrick's chest as he moved to the side and pulled her up against his body.

"This is what I miss when I'm away and there is no greater feeling than coming home to you and our brood."

"Daddy!" they heard on the other side of the bedroom door.

"Your timing is incredible!" Justine declared.

"Yeah, that's why we have three kids," Kenrick joked as he got out of the bed and pulled on shorts while giving Justine time to slip her gown back on before he opened the door.

"Mommy!" Erick shouted from the hallway.

Kenrick looked to her for confirmation.

"I'm good," she said.

As soon as he opened the door, both boys ran in and jumped up on the top of the comforter.

"Mommy, Jazzy is crying and won't stop. Grandma said she probably wants you," Ricky said.

Kenrick used the remote to open the curtains in the room, flooding it with daylight.

"Tell grandma I'll be down in a few minutes after I

grab a quick shower. It's okay to let the baby cry for a few minutes or she can take a bottle," she said. "Now, go get breakfast and I'll be right there," she added.

Both boys ran back through the door and Kenrick shook his head. "I guess this means we are officially up," he said.

"I guess so. I need to grab a shower and go tend to Jazzy before she bursts everyone's eardrums with her cries. She's use to the breasts and sometimes will not take a bottle."

Kenrick walked over to the bed. "I can relate. I happen to love your breasts, too," he quipped, grabbing for her.

"Oh, on you don't. No sex when our daughter is starving. I have enough time for a shower and that's it."

"Okay, but to be continued tonight?" he asked, almost on a plea.

"Absolutely."

Justine walked into their bathroom smiling like a woman who had just been thoroughly loved. She loved her life.

4 – Take a Knee

The house was filled with laughter as their families enjoyed the Thanksgiving evening. Kenrick looked around at the throngs of people who moved about in his house and he smiled. This is what family is supposed to be about, he thought to himself. He would always enjoy having his house filled with fun and laughter.

Kids ran around chasing each other while others enjoyed after dinner fun. The men retreated to one of the two media rooms to play pool and watch football while the kids were in the other playing games and watching movies. As usual, the women gathered in the kitchen and the family room that was off to the side of the kitchen. They never gathered in the living room which Justine had decorated in all white and gold. It was a room that was always off limits. They had more than enough rooms for sitting in their ten thousand square foot home.

The house consisted of ten bedrooms spread out amongst three separate wings of their house. The only people who slept in the main wing were him and Justine, their kids and the nanny. Along with the bedrooms, the house had twelve bathrooms, two media rooms, two kitchens and three great rooms or what some people called family rooms where sitting and lounging around were permitted and an indoor swimming pool. Teaching their kids how to swim was a priority for them both. They may not love the water, but in an emergency situation, they wanted to be sure their kids would be able to float and get themselves out of the water.

Outside, the grounds contained a full basketball court, two swimming pools, tennis courts and a playground that some thought was an amusement park.

Kenrick love their house and loved the privacy it afforded them living out in Alpine, New Jersey. They also owned a condominium in New York City and in Hawaii where they loved to vacation. They owned a home in Florida and one in Massachusetts. Though they had great wealth, they didn't flaunt it or abuse it. With the exception of their houses, they made sure to save a lot since he was planning to retire around the age of thirty-five, which was five years away. He didn't want to spend many more years than that running up and down the football field. He wanted time to enjoy the fruits of his labor.

Going toward the kitchen, Kenrick locked eyes with Justine and the fact that he was enamored by her was evident in his gaze. No one could mistake the love that was shared between them.

"The hour is getting late," Justine's uncle said.

"Aww, people are trickling out," Justine said.

"Don't act like you're not ready for us to leave. The kids are getting antsy and I'm sure it's past their bedtime. We're going to head back to the hotel for our flight out tomorrow morning."

Justine hugged her uncle and aunt who traveled all the way from Arizona to be with them for the holiday. Other family were also leaving in the morning, but some were staying through the weekend. She looked forward to entertaining the entire weekend.

Kenrick said goodbye to his brother and other family that were also leaving.

"We'll be over on Saturday to hang out," Josiah said. After he and Kenrick had found each other a few years back, they spent a lot of time together. At one point, Josiah and his family were thinking of moving to the west coast which didn't sit well with Kenrick. Knowing how important family was and how small theirs was, Josiah changed jobs after his company folded and with the help of Kenrick and some connections he had, he was able to land a lucrative job in computer programming and development and stayed close.

"Too bad your coach won't let the players play pickup games of football during the season or I'd get a game going with all this family Justine will have staying around for a few days," Josiah said as he and Kenrick walked out to his car.

"I know, but as soon as the season is over, I don't care how warm it is outside, we're gonna get some games popping," Kenrick said.

"I'm glad we found each other," Josiah said, finding himself still overwhelmed by their connection after growing up apart even though they knew about each other.

"So am I. You are why I have family," Kenrick said as they hugged. "See you on Saturday," he added and walked back to the house as Josiah got in his car with his family and drove off.

Kenrick went back into the house now that all those who were leaving were gone. Inside were Justine's parents and his kids who he knew were about to head to bed as Hannah led them up the stairs.

Not quite tired, he ventured into the media room where Justine's father sat enjoying a glass of wine.

"Well, another great Thanksgiving under our belt," Prentiss said when he and Kenrick were alone watching television in the media room after other family members had either gone home or gone to bed in another part of their expansive house.

"Yes, it was. I'm glad everyone was able to make it. I love having your family around," Kenrick said.

"It was good to see Paul and Minnie again. How is Andrea doing? I noticed she wasn't here this year."

Kenrick laid back in the soft black leather sectional and placed his feet up on the ottoman. He loved quiet nights like this one. Justine and her mother were in the kitchen talking and winding down for the night as Hannah helped the boys get dressed for bed. Jazzy, who still refused to go to sleep yet was in the kitchen already trying to talk up a storm at five months old.

"She's still in Paris. She's coming to town for Christmas this year and for the big game if we make it that far."

"Is that doubt I hear in your voice, son? Of course, you'll make it to the big game. This has been a record year for you and the team. Lots of big things have happened for you lately."

"Yeah, it has been a good year," Kenrick admitted.

"Especially the birth of that beautiful little girl. I can't seem to get enough of holding her. She's a happy little baby."

Kenrick couldn't agree more. Jazmine was his world every time she looked at him and grinned showing him her gums.

"That little girl could sneeze and make me jump to get her a tissue. I never knew the kind of love I have for her. I've heard other people say it, but I never knew it until I had a daughter, but there is something special about being the father of a girl. You want to love and protect them from everything in the world."

Prentiss looked over at Kenrick wondering if now was the time to have a conversation he'd tossed and turned over having. He didn't want to put a damper on the evening, but now that they were alone, he wanted to drop the weight of what he'd been carrying around for a while.

"I know how you feel. I've felt the same way about Justine her whole life. Listen, since we're alone, I'm hoping we can talk about something. I don't want it to get too serious, but thinking about Jazmine and how much I know you love her, I want to talk to you about that same kind of love that I have for my Justine."

Kenrick turned toward Prentiss and saw the serious look on his face. He reached for the remote and turned the television off.

"Sure, is something wrong?" he asked.

"Not really wrong, but something that's been weighing on me and has been for a long while," Prentiss said with a serious tone.

Kenrick nodded his head and waited. He'd never had a one on one serious conversation with Justine's father before. He considered him as close as any family member and loved that her father often called him son. The tone that he was getting from him alluded to something serious was on his mind. He scanned his history with Justine and couldn't think of an incident that would warrant her father stepping in.

He did his best every day to make sure Justine and his kids didn't want for anything. He made sure they knew he loved them and would do anything for them. He's given her a fairytale life and every single one of her wants and needs were met thanks to his career and his four-year, one hundred million dollar contract. He was already set to sign a new contract for five years at a hundred and fifty-million, securing a great life for his family for many years to come. Nothing was too great for them and whatever Justine wanted, she got. He couldn't imagine what was troubling her father.

"I've known you for nine years now and it's been nine great years. You love my daughter and she loves you. Everything she could ever want or need you make sure she has and I appreciate that, any father would. You and Justine gave us grandchildren and you have no idea the impact that's had on our lives. We love them so much and we love that you open your house to us to come and visit anytime we like."

Kenrick turned toward Prentiss so that they could talk more direct.

"Yet, there is some problem?" he asked.

"It's not a problem, but a father's concern. I love Justine and after having her, we found that my wife who almost died having her, couldn't have any more children which makes her extra special to us. You have a daughter now and I'm sure you would want the best for her. I believe you are what's best for her, but I have one issue I'd like to share with you and then I'm going to let it go."

"Okay," Kenrick said, curiously.

"Justine just had her third child and though there is no pressure, I'd like to know that my daughter's security is solidified. I would have preferred that she was married before having three children, but that didn't happen here. You kids did that backwards and you have every right to do that. I'm glad she waited until after she graduated from NYU in case she has dreams of having her own career one day after the kids are bigger. That doesn't ease my concern about your commitment to her. If you love her as much as you say and I know you do, why aren't you married?" Prentiss asked.

"Well, sir, I don't have a real answer for you other than we haven't talked about marriage."

Kenrick saw what looked like a confused look on Prentiss' face. He probably had a hard time that after nine years, the conversation of marriage never came up between them.

"You've never talked about marriage in the nine years you've been together or in the seven years since you started having children? As a father, that would give any man pause. I know a man in your position can have and do anything he wants and I'm looking out for my daughter."

Kenrick tried to pick his words to explain carefully. The last thing he wanted was for there to be bad blood between them.

"I do love Justine with everything that's in me and in my own way, I am very committed to her and our kids. They are my life and they will forever be my life. A piece of paper won't change that. They will have me forever."

"If that's the case, then why not marry her? What's preventing you from doing it?" Prentiss asked.

"Have you talked to Justine about this?" Kenrick asked. He was concerned that Justine and her father had discussed this and she didn't bring it up to him.

They shared everything and never kept secrets.

"No, I haven't. My wife and I have talked about it and she has the same concern. I want you to understand that I'm looking out for my daughter and I'm concerned that she'll have more babies, which we have no problem with, but it locks up her life, but not yours. Not that you would, but you could walk away any time you want to and where would that leave her?"

Kenrick was uncomfortable. Thoughts of his mother leaving him as a child and his father going off the deep end and all of that turning his life upside down came to the forefront of his mind. He wondered if Justine had talked of leaving him if he didn't marry her and not discussed it with him. He felt like her father was coming out of left field with this talk of marriage like there was something he needed to be worried about.

"I'm never leaving Justine and I would never leave my kids. I know what that feels like and I love them too much to ever do that," he explained.

Prentiss reached over and patted his shoulder to make sure the moment wasn't a tense one.

"I hear you, son. I believe that and I know it's coming from your heart. You have a daughter now. I want you to think as if this were Jazmine we were talking about instead of Justine and think about how you'd feel and how you'd handle it. I don't know much about your life before Justine and I'm sorry if your life has left you with doubts about love, relationships and marriage, but this is my daughter we're talking about. If you love her and you plan to love her for the rest of your life, then you should think about making it official."

Prentiss stood to leave.

"I don't know what to say. I feel like I should say that I'm sorry that I'm not moving at the pace you'd like," Kenrick said, getting more defensive than he wanted.

"Son, I'm not trying to tell you how to live your life or what you should be doing. I'm sharing with you my feelings because Justine to me is your Jazmine to you and I see how much you love that little girl. If you were in my shoes, you would be asking these questions, too."

Kenrick nodded his head in agreement and he also knew that there were things that Prentiss didn't understand because he didn't know the whole story.

"Sir, there are things about my life that have impacted me that I can't go into right now and maybe I do have a problem with committing that much. The only thing I can tell you is that I love Justine and I would never, ever hurt her," he said.

"I hear you, Kenrick and I understand. I will say that you know how to reach me if you ever need or want to talk about anything. I love you like a son and you know that and I don't want this conversation to cause any problems. I love Justine just as you do and I want the best for her and that best is you, but it should be all of you, not just what you are willing to give for now."

Kenrick stood with him.

"I understand and I'm thankful that you see me as a son. You have always treated me like one and I appreciate that. I promise you, I will think about everything you said and I appreciate the offer to talk at any time," he said.

"That offer stands forever with no expiration date," Prentiss said. "Now, I'm going to go in search of my beautiful wife to get her to relax. She loves cooking for family and sometimes she fails to wind down at the end of the day. Thanks for having us and again, anytime you want to talk, you know how to reach me," Prentiss said and then left the room.

Kenrick was left alone with his own thoughts. His mind went back to his mother who never really wanted or loved him and a father who hated him just because he lived. Due to their treatment, he didn't see commitment the way others did. He saw his own parents never commit to each other and never committed to raising him. There was a part of him deep down that was afraid to go to the next level with Justine. Even though they had the perfect love, he felt like he was always waiting for the other shoe to drop and one day she'd be gone. From his mother, he learned that women liked to be free to leave if they chose and he didn't want Justine to stay with him out of obligation if they got married. Where the thought came from he didn't know because that was in no way Justine. Shaking off any bad thoughts, he straightened up the room before turning out the light and going in search of Justine. He had a lot to think about.

5 – Take a Knee

"Kenrick? Where are you?" Josiah asked as soon as he answered the phone.

"I'm in my car about to pull up."

"Is it just you or are you accompanied by your entourage?"

Kenrick knew Josiah was both joking and serious at the same time. He was known for the large number of guys who typically followed him wherever he went and that didn't include his security detail. He liked having people around, something he missed growing up without much family. Without having that family, he enjoyed connecting with friends he'd made from college and they loved hanging around him. That wasn't on his mind tonight. This time, he needed to talk to his brother alone.

"Just me. I told you this was a night out for you and me and no one else. You did leave Naomi at home, right?" Kenrick asked.

He loved Josiah's wife and kids, but there was a time

and a place to have everyone around and a night at the pool hall wasn't it.

"My wife is at home cuddled up with the twins watching some Disney movie for the hundredth time," Josiah said.

"I'm surprised she let you out tonight!" Kenrick joked.

"Bro, don't get it twisted – when I'm at home with my family, it's the first place I want to be, not the last. I love being up under my wife after spending a day in the rat race I call a career in computers. I love what I do, but nothing compares to the time I spend with my family. You're not one to talk. I know how you are with Justine and the kids."

With one big difference, Kenrick thought to himself, but didn't speak it out loud. The word marriage still lingered in the air after his talk a few weeks ago with Justine's father.

"I'm about to park. I'll see you in a few," he said.

Kenrick disconnected the call and parked in the parking space that belong to the bar owner, Paul, left vacant especially for him. Paul was like a father to him. When he had home games and wanted a place to go where he wasn't mobbed, he chose the pool hall where Paul let him use one of the private rooms to play. Unless he gave permission himself, no one else was allowed in the room. Tonight, he wanted to talk to Josiah and wanted to do so in his place of solitude.

Getting out of the car, he grabbed his cell phone and sent one quick text to Justine to let her know he'd be late because he was going to play a few games of pool with his brother. She was his everything and though a lot of people had major expectations of him every day, she only expected his love and devotion for her and their kids and that's the one thing he always wanted to make sure she knew she had from him. His life growing up wasn't the best, but he wanted his kids to know he would always be around for them, making them a priority.

Typing in another message, he read it twice before sending.

'You are my everything and I love you to the moon and back.'

Kenrick smiled after sending it knowing that she would remember that he'd said the exact same thing on their second date years ago. As he opened the back door to the pool hall, his phone vibrated. He smiled wider seeing her 'ditto', the same response she sent him back then.

Going inside, he looked around for Paul, the one man in his life since he was a teenager who showed him love like a father would. When they visually connected, Paul rushed to escort him to the private room before others in the main room spotted him and then he'd never get a game in without being interrupted.

"Thanks, as usual. Have you spotted my brother? He called me saying he was here," Kenrick said, removing his jacket and already reaching for his favorite pool cue.

"He's out at the bar. I'll let him know you're here. Your usual?" Paul asked.

"Usual drink, but for food, bring me some wings, three flavors, barbecue, old bay and parmesan garlic. Add in a big basket of onion rings and I think I'll be set for the night. How's Minnie? I'm going to stop by the house tomorrow. It's decorating time and I want to start pulling everything out."

"You know you don't have to do that every year. We can pay someone to do the decorating. I'm sure you have other things you need to do," Paul said.

"Nonsense. I love to do I and it gives Minnie a chance to tell me about all the things you've been eating that you're not suppose to eat. Besides, I love doing it. When I'm on break from a game, going to the house is top on my agenda," Kenrick said.

Paul's heart swelled with love for his son. Though he wasn't his biological son, Kenrick was the son he wished they could have had but didn't have. One of the best days of his life was the day he found Kenrick as a young teen sleeping in the back of his truck.

"I know. Minnie will be excited to see you. We had a good time at Thanksgiving dinner. I know you have Christmas day brunch at your house, but Minnie and I would like to have you over a few days before Christmas. Andrea will be home and Minnie has all kinds of things planned," Paul said.

"We'll be there. I can't wait to see her and she'd finally get to see Jazzy in person."

"Let Minnie know, when you go by the house, that you'll be able to make it."

"Wouldn't miss it," Kenrick said. He loved Paul and

41

Minnie and there wasn't anything he wouldn't do to put a smile on their faces. If it weren't for them, he wouldn't have the life he had now. They were his heroes.

"Good. Let me get your food ordered. Lemonade, wings and onion rings it is," Paul said.

Kenrick would love to have his usual beer, but he never drank when he drove himself around and never right before a game. His last game before the holiday was coming up."

"What's up Kenrick!" Josiah said coming into the room and closing the door behind him.

"Hey, bro. How long have you been here?"

"Long enough to know you're late," he laughed. "I'll let you repay me with all of the fried shrimp and wings I just ordered on your tab!" he quipped.

"I got you. Ready for a few games?" Kenrick asked.

"Of course. How often do I get to play a game that I can beat my little brother in? Are you ready for the big game this week?"

"I am. It's always good to play at home. There's nothing like the hometown fans, win or lose, they love us. I do expect we'll hold on to our winning streak this week."

"How are Justine and the kids, especially my little niece? I have been meaning to stop by the house since Thanksgiving, but I've been crazy busy at work. I know Naomi was there earlier this week so that the kids could play."

"I was out of town, but Justine told me she had been

by. She loves when they can get together."

Kenrick beamed thinking about his family at home. When he left them, Justine was feeding Jazzy and the boys were playing a board game with her parents who were in town for the game and staying with them. He was glad that things were not awkward between him and Prentiss after their talk on Thanksgiving. Even though they had been in contact since then, the subject never came up again.

"They're great and Jazzy has reeled me in, hook, line and sinker, man. I swear looking at that beautiful little girl makes everything in my world good, even though the world is crazy right now," Kenrick said.

"I hear you. All the hate and disparity. What's the deal with taking a knee this week? Will the team be doing it again? Last week was crazy, but thankfully the majority of the fans are supportive, but that was an away game."

"True. It would be great if people realized it's not about disrespecting the flag or even the game; it's about our right to take a knee in this free country to support a cause that's dear to us all and that is seeing and being treated as equals. As far as I know, the team is taking the knee this week and if so, then I will too."

"This is all about that one player on your team who took a stand early in the season and now is being ostracized. I respect what he's trying to do, call attention to the mistreatment of other black men. I'm glad your coach and team owners are supportive."

"No one means any disrespect, but at least, it has

people talking and that's a good start. I work for a great club and their support means everything."

"True," Kenrick said. "Speaking of taking a knee, I wanted to talk to you about something.

Kenrick grabbed the pool balls and rack and prepared the table for their first game. He was about to take his first shot when the door opened and Paul walked in with a tray of food.

"Wow, we must be hungry tonight!" Josiah said and took the tray from Paul's hands.

"If you need anything else, let me know. The kitchen is open as long as you're here," he said and walked out.

"Paul is a great man," Kenrick said.

"You told me bits and pieces about how you came to live with them, but I want all the details," Josiah said.

"Well, I think I told you I met the in my freshman year in high school when I ran away from the foster home and ended up sleeping in the back of his flatbed truck. When I woke up and saw him standing over me, I was about to bolt. All I could think about were those whippings I took from my foster father and Paul was a large, powerful figure. Instead of running me off, he invited me in to have breakfast with him and his wife. They asked me a million questions about why I was sleeping in the back of the truck. His wife had seen me there two nights before and still, she didn't demand that I get off of their property. That morning, she sent Paul out to bring me inside. They have always been good to me and I owe them everything. Paul has always treated me like a son."

As soon as he said the words, he looked over at Josiah knowing they were thinking the same thing.

"Our father wasn't the greatest, was he?" Josiah asked. "I mean, it's a miracle you and I found each other. We still have two sisters and a brother out in the world someplace."

Kenrick saw the solemn look on his brother's face which mirrored how he was also feeling.

"I know and I intend to find them. I wanted to tell you that the private detective that I hired to find you is all over this case. He assures me that he can find just about anyone. We don't have a lot of information, but he was able to find you for me. Our poppa was a rolling stone and he never cared a lick about any of us, but that doesn't mean we can't get to know each other. There are five of us, that we know of and four different mothers, which is crazy," Kenrick said glumly.

"He was a horrible father to me and I know what he did to you, but that was a long time ago. Life is different for you now just like it is for me. I don't want to always look back and remember. It's too painful and I know it is for you, too. How are you doing dealing with the past?" Josiah asked.

Kenrick took his first shot and thought about the question. Every day, he still lived with the memories of a father who didn't want him and a mother who left him with a father who mistreated him as payback for his mother leaving them. His childhood still plagued him and he wished he could leave it in the past where it belonged. He knew that Josiah was able to do that, but for him, it was still a struggle.

"I still have my struggles, but I think they're getting better," Kenrick said, hoping he could convince himself of his own words.

"You are one of the highest paid football players in the league, you have a fantastic, beautiful woman and three kids who love you like crazy, though you may end up coming in second place when it comes to my niece. Naomi and I have been thinking about trying for a girl to help soften those boys and me. I think Justine having Jazzy is pushing her to try again soon. You have an incredible life despite your upbringing. Delight in that and let the past go."

Josiah's words rang loud in his head because it was something he found himself always trying to do without succeeding. He was appreciative of everything he had and Josiah was right, it was all in spite of his childhood.

"My family is everything to me, but sometimes I feel like I'm coming up short in giving them all of me," Kenrick said, sitting the pool cue down and sitting at the table in front of the food. He picked a few wings up and some onion rings and prepared to pour his heart out to his brother.

The day the private investigator found Josiah was the happiest day of his life. Since the first day they met in person, they have been inseparable. The only hinderance was at the time, Josiah was living and working in Chicago, far from him. A year after meeting, he talked Josiah into moving so that they could be closer and he helped him land a position in New York. There is nothing he wouldn't do for his brother, the only family he was able to locate so far. He looked up as Josiah came over and sat across from him.

"What do you mean? They know you love them?"

"The reason I wanted to talk to you and what I meant when I said I wanted to talk to you about a different kind of taking a knee, is because you have a background similar to mine and unlike you, I still have trust issues."

"Is this about you and Justine?" Josiah asked.

"It is. Her father and I had a conversation after everyone left on Thanksgiving. It was pretty deep. He didn't want me to think that he was pressuring me into anything when it comes to a commitment to Justine, but that's what I took from it and I understand where he's coming from. Justine has given me three beautiful children and I swear there isn't a better woman out here than her. My not asking her to marry me yet has nothing to do with her, but everything to do with me," Kenrick admitted.

"I hear you and I understand. What you went through, no child should ever have had to go through, but you survived. You can't help the uncaring people your parents turned out to be or the horrible foster parents you ended up with. You told me your life turned around once you moved in with Paul and his wife and that's what you should focus on when you think about family. Them, me and my family and Justine, her family and your kids."

Kenrick shook his head, understanding.

"What am I afraid of then? Why can't I do the right thing? Why haven't I done the right thing all these years? You know, three kids ago? I knew I didn't want anyone after meeting Justine. She was it for me and she's never complained about our life. I know she would like to be married liked other women and I want that, too."

"Do you think she'll end up leaving you one day which is why you don't make the ultimate commitment, leaving her free and clear to leave? What about the kids? Whose idea was it to have the kids? Yours or hers?" Josiah asked. He wasn't trying to be crude or harsh, but he needed Kenrick to think in terms of reality and not what's been clouding up his mind.

"That was all me. I've never told anyone this, not even Justine, but I wanted these kids badly because I didn't have a family growing up until Paul and Minnie. On the surface, I wanted her to have the kids just in case she wasn't happy for some reason and I knew she wouldn't leave because we had kids. Now, when I say it out loud, it sounds selfish."

"Kenrick, it's okay to feel that way. How much about your past have you actually shared with Justine?" Josiah asked.

"Not as much as I should have. It's hard to talk about and I don't want that misery creeping into our lives."

"I understand, but until you talk to her about everything, you won't be able to let it go for good and move forward. Justine deserves to be your wife and not just your girlfriend or the mother of your children. I know she may not have ever brought it up, but don't you think that she would love to know that level of love and commitment from you?"

Kenrick nodded. He wasn't blind to Justine's reaction every time she hears about one of her friends getting engaged or when she's at the games and there is another player who proposed to his girlfriend.

"I know she would which is why I wanted to talk to you about something that happened. At a recent game, when she was finally able to come out after having Jazzy, one of the wives on the team made a comment to her about having three kids with me and why I hadn't married her yet. Justine didn't tell me about the conversation. One of the other wives mentioned it to her husband and he brought it to my attention in the locker room during practice recently. He wanted me to know that his wife saw the look on Justine's face that wasn't a pleasant one. Justine didn't get upset in front of the other wives, but she excused herself and when this player's wife followed her to the ladies room, she thought she heard Justine crying and left her alone."

Even now, Kenrick balled his hands into fists, angry about what Justine had to encounter. He knew some of the player's wives could be witches.

"I see. Did Justine's father say anything else during your chat? You said it got pretty deep," Josiah asked.

"He made a comment about how many more kids were we going to have without something more permanent. Her father has always been good to me, but at that moment, I wanted to tell him it was none of his business what goes on between Justine and I, but I didn't. I let him have his say. They're here for the game, visiting with us and staying at the house for a few days. After we talked, it bothered me for the rest of the night. He has to know that I love her and would never hurt her or discard her and my kids."

"I don't think that's his point. Think about this. What if Jazzy were a woman around Justine's age when she met you and she came home saying she met a guy who she loved and who loved her. For years after that, she keeps coming home saying she's pregnant with another one of his babies, but no marriage. Wouldn't you want better for Jazzy? You wouldn't want some guy to keep knocking your daughter up and not marrying her. I know if I had a daughter, I would find that unacceptable and I would do exactly what her father did and pull the guy up about it. They love you, but they love their daughter first and they want more for her than to just be your baby making machine. It's not fair to her and you know it."

Kenrick held his head down and thought for a few minutes before he spoke.

"She's much more than that to me."

Kenrick had no problem telling the world that she was his everything.

"I know that, you know that and I'm sure everyone around you knows that, but you have to show and prove, little brother. I see your passion for the taking a knee movement when the real cause you should be taking a knee for is right in front of your face. If Justine is all you will ever want, then take the knee. If you know you can't live without her for the rest of your life, then take the knee. If you're ready to let go of all of your insecurities about being anything like your mother or our dad, then take the knee. Take the knee because you know your family deserves all of you. You have me, Paul and his wife and all that family on Justine's side. You have love being poured on you all the time. You are loved, brother. We are all committed to loving you no matter what. Whatever happened in your past and I'm sure there are parts you still haven't told me and that's fine, but it's time to let it go and trust that what you and Justine have is forever. It won't be broken like your life was in the past. Your life with Justine is happy and healthy and so will your life once you make her your wife. Think about it while I take this pool shot, the beginning of showing you what I'm good at. You may be the best on the field, but I'm the best on this playing field," Josiah said and stood.

Kenrick smiled, happy he had his brother to talk to. His advice meant everything and he was right – it was time to let go of the past that was keeping him from the future, not only he deserved, but Justine and their kids deserved. He shook off the depression that threatened to rear its ugly head and perked up to take advantage of time with his brother.

"I'm the best at everything!" Kenrick declared and joined him at the pool table.

"Okay, mister best at everything. When you go home tonight, be the best at laying your entire past out to your lovely woman and release that drama from your spirit and from your life. Even if we never find our siblings, we have each other and we're going into our future scathed free. Agreed?" Josiah asked.

Kenrick smiled and nodded.

"Agreed."

6 – Take a Knee

Justine checked on the baby one last time before heading into her bedroom to finish packing Kenrick's bag. Even though his next game was a home game, the coach liked for the team to stay at the same hotel where transportation would be provided to take them all to the game. He wanted to be sure there were no distractions and everyone arrived on time.

The boys had been down for over an hour and her parents had retired to the guest wing of their house where they could stay up late and have snacks prepared by the house staff without waking the kids. She was expecting Kenrick home soon after he left earlier to spend some time with his brother. She loved that he and Josiah were forming an unbreakable bond after meeting each other as adult men. Often, without that connection being made as boys, it's hard for men to develop that type of bond later, but they had. There was a lot about his life she still didn't know and she assumed he would share it when he was ready.

For years, Kenrick suffered from horrible nightmares that had him waking in the middle of the night, completely soaked from sweat. She had learned how to help calm him down, allowing him to get back to sleep, but he still never wanted to talk to her about his deep-rooted problems. Whatever the issue was, she was terrified every time he woke up screaming and with a petrified look on his face. She only knew surface information about his past, but she knew there had to be more, much more and whatever it was, it was bad.

Kenrick had been hurt when he was younger and other than telling her about how terrible his birth parents had been, he hadn't shared much more about his life. By the time they met, he was living with Paul and Minnie who were like parents to him. There has always been a part of him that she had been unable to reach, but that didn't diminish her love for him.

Kenrick loved her and their kids with a passion that she'd only seen in her own father. Now that their oldest son, Ricky was old enough, Kenrick was going to volunteer to help coach his pee-wee baseball team. Though he loved playing football, he wanted Ricky to do something in sports that was less wear and tear on the body. She loved how he looked forward to more bonding opportunities with all of the kids.

Walking into the bedroom's walk-in closet, which was the size of most large bedrooms, she pulled out the suit she knew he wanted to wear to the game by his favorite designer, Hermès. It was a design made especially for him in his favorite navy-blue which patches of plaid. She found a black shirt for him to wear under it and pulled out his own brand of dress shoe called, *Kenly*, a new line that was sitting at the top of the charts in the men's clothing line for the season. His knack for dressing kept him in the headlines and she loved seeing him dress up. Besides being the handsomest guy, she'd ever met, her man could wear a suit and make it his own. Her thoughts turned to the day they met and how handsome he was. Though he towered over her five-foot-seven height, standing at six-foot-four, he was the perfect height for her. She believed tall men made a woman feel even more protected.

On that particular day, he was with friends in Times Square looking like an Adonis. He had on his college football jersey and some denim jeans that curved with his sexy bowlegs. A lot of girls loved dark, chocolate men, but she believed light skin would ever be in for her and Kenrick was light, gorgeous and reminded her of her favorite *Grey's Anatomy* actor, Jesse Williams. They could be twins they looked so much alike. From day one, he was the guy for her and they had been inseparable since that moment. She loved that they were able to enjoy each other before his career took off. She loved him before and knew that she would continue to do so until the end of time.

Pulling out accessories, she then went into the bathroom and pulled out the toiletries he would need.

"Hello beautiful!"

Justine turned at the sound of Kenrick's voice. She shivered when she saw him standing in the bedroom doorway looking like a sexy model in his all black attire of dress pants and open collar black shirt. It was the perfect picture of him against their beige bedroom walls. Peering through the v-opening in the shirt was a think coat of light brown hair on his chest. She loved rubbing her fingers over the soft hair there.

"Hi, baby. I didn't hear you come in," she said.

"You were deep in thought. I stopped in to check on the kids first and it's a good thing I did. Erick was practically on the floor. I'm glad he loves that bottom bunk or we'd have to keep him in a crib for years. He's a wild sleeper," he laughed.

"Yes, he is, just like his father," Justine said coming up to Kenrick and leaning up to prepare for the powerful kiss she always knew to expect from him.

"How long has Jazzy been down?" he asked moving about the room, removing his clothes.

"She'll be up any minute now. I was trying not to go to sleep too early knowing she would wake up for her night feeding. At almost six months old, I'll be glad when she sleeps the entire night."

"She likes being up this hour which is why I call her our little blocker. She knows what's on her daddy's mind when he comes home at night and finds his gorgeous wife walking around in a sexy, satin robe."

"That's another reason I love waiting up for you," Justine said, adding a hint of sexiness to her voice.

Before he could respond, Kenrick heard his fussy daughter let out a cry that could wake up the dead.

"Sounds like she's up now."

Justine walked toward the bedroom door. She gave Hannah a few days off since she would spend the day with them at Kenrick's next home football game.

"She is always on time," she laughed.

"Do you have milk pumped in the fridge already?" Kenrick asked.

"Yes. They're dated and timed."

"Let me feed her. You know I love feeding her and bonding with her when I'm home."

"Are you sure? I'm sure you want some down time," Justine said.

"I'm sure and I'll get plenty of downtime, but nothing compares to quiet time with my little lady. I'll get her changed and take her down with me. Once I put her back to sleep, I'm going to come in here and work on putting you to sleep in my favorite way," Kenrick said slyly, winking to be sure Justine knew his intention.

"That, I'm always ready for. While you're doing that, I'm going to get a hot bath. It's not often all three of them are taken care of and I can get a free moment to take a bath. Even my mom and dad went to bed early. The kids wore them out," she said.

Kenrick pulled Justine in his arms and kissed her passionately before releasing her.

"I could use a little wearing out," he laughed. "Why don't you go do that and have some time to yourself while I take care of our daughter with the powerful lungs. Perhaps you'll still be in the tub when I come back and I can join you in there," he said with smoky, erotic tone in his voice.

"Offer me a good time and I'm there. Tell our daughter to help me out and go back to sleep quickly. Mommy needs some daddy time, too," she said smiling.

Jazzy screamed louder.

"I guess that's my cue to hurry up with her bottle." Kenrick kissed Justine one last time. "I'll see you shortly," he said.

"I'll be in the tub wet and waiting for you."

Kenrick waited long enough to watch the woman of his dreams saunter into their bathroom and then turned his attention to his daughter. Going across the hall, he tried to soothe her as he picked her up by rubbing her back the way she loved.

"Hi, baby girl. It's daddy to the rescue. I promise I will change you with lightning speed and then get you that bottle you're hollering for. Give daddy a minute," he said softly. He laid her down on the changing table and swiftly got her changed and back in his arms. Her crying turned to fun time as she bounced and giggled in his arms as he made his way down the stairs and into the kitchen.

"You know I cherish this time with you, Jazzy. There were times when I was younger when most guys would never dream of talking about having children, but that's exactly what I did. I didn't have much love in my life when I was little and I couldn't wait to grow up and give my love to my own children. The days that you and your brothers were born were the happiest days of my life. You, though, were extra special. I had no idea I could have this much love for a little girl," he said directly to her.

Kenrick smiled when she quieted and focused on his face as he spoke while warming up her milk. His heart melted a little more each time he looked at her and she patted him on the face. Only he knew that her little gesture meant the world to him. He forever wanted to love and respect of his little girl.

"I can't wait to play tea party with you and let you polish my nails and put barrettes in my hair. I will be on the front row for all of your events from ballet recitals, to gymnastic matches and even karate if you want to do that. As your father, I will love, cherish and support you and never will I allow anyone to mistreat you on my watch. If they try, you tell them who your father is and that I will pounce them if they don't treat you with the utmost respect. Deal?" he said.

Jazmine laughed out loud when he smiled at her, though he was serious. When she looked at the bottle in his hand, she started to whimper, preparing to let out a new cry. Gone was her delight at seeing her daddy, replaced by her need to feed.

"Okay, I got it. Daddy talks too much when you're hungry."

Kenrick fed her and kept his eyes on hers as he continued to talk. He knew that Justine loved to breast feed and bond and his favorite times when he was home was when she let him spend time feeding her. These are times he would never forget and he hoped his daughter would remember them too. He wanted her to recognize his voice and know his face over everyone else's. He was her protector, her first love and he wanted to be sure she knew he was always going to be there.

"Daddy loves you Jazzy," he said and quieted while she ate.

His thoughts turned to his conversations with Prentiss and Josiah where they compared his love for his daughter with the love Prentiss had for Justine and they were right, he wanted more for Jazmine than a man who had no problem giving her baby after baby, but no real commitment in the form of marriage. Here he was telling his own daughter that he would hurt any man who didn't treat her right and yet, he was doing that exact same thing. Josiah's words rang out in his head – take the knee, take the knee, take the knee!

7 – Take a Knee

Justine lost track of time in the tub surrounded by lighted candles as soft music wafted through the speakers in the wall. This night couldn't be more perfect with the house quiet and soon, some romance with her sexy man. Adding to the ambience, she was glad she'd turned the bathroom light off before getting into the tub.

"Hey, you," Kenrick said entering the bathroom.

"Hey back. I just refilled the tub with fresh water and soap once I heard you putting Jazzy back in her crib. How did she eat?" she asked.

"Like a linebacker. She sure was hungry and like a linebacker, as soon as she was done, she was out like a light. I pet her back like you told me to until she burped and then she really settled down."

Kenrick placed the baby monitor on the counter so that they could hear if Jazzy woke up. Removing his clothes, he stepped in the shower to wash off the dirt of the day before exiting and joining Justine in the large tub made for two.

When he looked at the original plans when the house was being built, he made a few requests, but the main one was how he wanted the bathroom designed so that they could bathe and shower together. He knew there would be times when that would be the only quiet spot in their house.

He slid in behind Justine as she moved up to accommodate his six-foot-four frame.

"So, our daughter knocked one back and is out like a light?" Justine asked.

"She is. We had a few struggles with the bottle because I'm sure she was expecting you, but I prevailed and she sucked until the last drop. I cleaned her up and even put on a new onesie before putting her to bed. I think I handled that pretty good," he said.

"You're getting good at your daddy role. I can tell she knows your voice because anytime I have her in my arms and she hears your voice, she starts squirming around looking for you. You spoil her," Justine said.

"I enjoy spoiling her and it's only just begun. How was your day?" he asked, cuddling up. He relaxed when Justine began massaging his legs.

"Well, I was able to get out to the hair and nail salon earlier and I selected some new decorations for the interior designer who's coming to decorate the house for the Christmas holiday. Can you believe Christmas is in two weeks? Time is moving so fast. Soon, we'll be sending our kids off to college and Jazzy will be bringing home her first boyfriend. Are you ready for that?" she kidded.

"I'll never be ready for that. No man will ever be good enough for my baby girl," he said. As soon as the words left his mouth, Kenrick thought again about the conversation he'd had with her father and with his brother. Everything he said seemed to bring those talks to light. The reality stung him like a mean, nasty bee. He had unfounded reservations, but not anymore. He'd kept his deepest, darkest secrets from her, but not anymore.

"How was playing pool with Josiah?" Justine asked.

"It was great. We ate more wings than I'll ever admit and we had a chance to talk or at least he let me talk and he listened."

"Is everything okay?" Justine asked. She knew that Kenrick had been distracted by something lately and figured when he was ready to talk to her about it he would. They had always been good about talking even though there as a big part of him that he had always been hesitant about sharing. She never pushed, but allowed him to know that she was here anytime he needed her.

"Sort of," Kenrick said. Now that they had some quiet time alone, it was time he shared his innermost secrets with her.

"What's wrong, babe? You know I'm always here."

Kenrick kissed the back of her neck and then placed a soft open-mouthed kiss on her shoulder before pulling her back even closer to his body. He needed her close as he relived a part of his past that he didn't even want to think about, let alone talk about.

"I know and I love you so much for that. There are some things about my life I haven't shared with you. I know when we first met, I was hard to understand and a few times I thought you were going to leave me because I was being difficult to be involved with."

Justine caressed his hands, comforting him for whatever he was going through. She needed him to know that from day one, she was always all in with him.

"I wasn't going to leave you. When I told you I loved you even after our second date, I meant it and I still do. That love means I stick around through the good and the bad," she said.

"I was mean to you sometimes back then, without any reason other than I didn't know how to love or be in love."

"You learned and that's all that matters. No love is perfect and we weren't then, but we sure are now," Justine said smiled.

"Yes, we are. You know I have some fears, right? There are some things that happened to me that I have never been able to shake. Things I probably should have gotten counseling for years ago, but I didn't."

"Aren't the players required to go through counseling sessions?" Justine asked.

"Yes, but that's all about playing the game. It wasn't really a deep dive into bottomless issues, especially those that are family related," Kenrick explained.

Justine exhaled, preparing herself to hear about those demons that kept him up some nights. Whatever they were, she was going to be strong, supportive and loving.

"You want to talk about them now?" she asked.

"Yes, if you think this is a good time."

"Anytime is a good time if you need to talk. Tell me about it, about your childhood. I'm here for you."

Kenrick kissed her quickly and held on to his nerves because he was about to lay it all out for her.

"Well, I told you my mother left when I was a little boy, but what I didn't tell you was that when she left, she left me in a house for four days by myself when I was five years old. I was in a house with barely any food and the electricity had been shut off, so days were cold and nights were freezing and creepy," he proclaimed.

Kenrick felt Justine stiffen in front of him. He rubbed her arms to soothe her. He knew she was thinking the same thing that he had thought each time he saw his own sons – he knew how small and defenseless a child is at five years old.

"My goodness," Justine said.

"I know. Anyway, she called herself leaving me with my father who had disappeared to spend time with one of his other women. He was married to my mother, but she then found out he had a child older than me and one younger than me and she went off after finding out he was spending his time between the three of them. That last time, the last day I saw her, she was horrible to me. She told me when she looked at me, I reminded her of my cheating father and she would beat me and slap me around all because I looked like him and when he wasn't with her, she knew he was with another woman. That last day was the last straw for her when the electricity was cut off. She tried to reach my father and couldn't. That made her angrier. She told me she never wanted me. She only wanted my father and thought having a child would domesticate him. It didn't work."

"Clearly not," Justine said. "I know Josiah is one of your siblings, but who is the other?" she asked.

"That's the million-dollar question. We still don't know. I know it's a girl, but nothing else. We also found out that over the past ten years or so, he's had two other children. I have a private eye looking for them, just as he found Josiah."

"That's good. That also means you have a brother and sister that are only a few years older than our kids? How wild is that?" she asked excited.

"Yes. I'm anxious to meet them and I hope their lives are better than mine and Josiah's was. Anyway, my mom finally reached my father the day she left me and told him that she left me at the house and that he needed to get home to get me because she wasn't coming back. That day, she left and never came back. I guess he didn't believe her because he didn't come home for five days and found me in the house alone. The house was already a mess, but I made an even bigger mess. I can still remember looking around for food to eat. I was dirty and hadn't bathed. I had to ramble through the fridge and the cabinets to find food to eat and there were bugs and mice everywhere. By the time he got there, it was doubly nasty. The bad part was he blamed me. He kept shouting he blamed me for being born. He beat me so bad that night, it took weeks for the scars to heal. The ones on my legs and arms never really healed all the way which is why I tried covering them with tattoos."

Justine rubbed on his outer leg where she knew one of the scars was.

"Poor baby," she said as her voice cracked. She couldn't begin to image the hurt and pain.

"It was horrible, but I survived. After that, my dad would leave for a day here and there and the neighbors would look after me, making sure I got to school. One lady kept clean clothes for me at her house and when my father made me walk over to her house in the morning as he left out to go someplace, she would put me in the tub and put clean clothes on me. He said he was out looking for my mother, but he was actually going between a lot of different women, all as it turned out were ladies of the night. I didn't know it before, but that's what my mother and Josiah's mother were when he met them. They were walking the streets making money and they thought this handsome guy was about something, but turned out to be nothing. Once they found out, they no longer wanted their kids."

Justine sloshed around in the water as she turned around to straddle his lap. She wanted to be able to comfort him as he told her about his painful past. She wanted him to be able to look in her face for comfort.

"Did Josiah grow up in foster care like you did?" she asked as she caressed his face which was taut with pain from what his mind was reliving.

"No, he lived with his mother's relatives and though his life wasn't perfect, it wasn't as bad as mine. His mother eventually left him, too, but he was left with family. My father abused me in ways I have been unable to tell anyone about other than Josiah. I've been afraid to tell you because I didn't want you to look at me differently or with disgust because of where I came from. I figured as long as you didn't know, you would continue to love the guy you met in Times Square nine years ago," he professed.

Justine reached up and cupped his face in her hands, drawing his head up until he looked directly in her eyes.

"Nothing would make me love you less, never. What happened to you should never have happened, but you made it through," she said.

"I did and that was because of Paul and Minnie. After years of abuse by my father burning me with lit cigarettes, beating me with anything he could get his hands on to locking me in closets for days without food and then beating me for wetting myself after days of being in thee, I was finally taken away from him. What should have been an improvement turned out to be worse. I think I was about ten by then and I was placed into foster care. That life was brutal until one day during my first year of high school, I came home late one day from school after staying for tryouts for the football team. My foster father beat me and threw me around the house like a rag doll. He told me the only reason I was there was because of the check. He beat me so bad, I couldn't lie down in the bed that night to go to sleep. The bed really wasn't a bed as much as it was an air mattress that seldom had any air in it. I had two pairs of pants and three shirts that I had to change up every day and I washed them by hand to keep them clean. In spite of that, I got good grades. I saw that as my only way out of the system and then there was sports. I hadn't played much, but I loved watching football. The day I tried out for the team, the coach was so impressed with me that he didn't assign me to the junior varsity team, he assigned me to the varsity team. I was excited until I got home and suffered at the hands of my foster father."

Kenrick smiled when Justine reached for a dry wash cloth and wiped his forehead. Though it was hot due to the steam from the tub, he was also sweating as he thought back over his past and vivid images of his life came into view.

"I'm here, baby," she said. "I'm here and you're here with me where there is an abounding amount of love for you, unconditional love," Justin shared.

"I know baby and I love you for loving me the way you do," he said and looked down.

Justine reached out with her hand and raised his head again.

"Keep your eyes on me so that you know through all

of this, I'm right here with you."

Kenrick nodded held on to her waist as she straddled him while he continued with his story.

"The next morning I told him that I made the team and he told me to quit because he wasn't giving me any money to play any sport. In fact, he told me he wanted me to quit school and find a job to help out and if the people from social services asked me about quitting school, I needed to tell them it was my idea so that he wouldn't get in trouble and lose the money he got for me each month. I didn't want to quit and I told him the money he got was to take care of me. That set him off and he came after me. I ran out that day and I still went to school. That evening, I snuck in the house through a window I knew didn't have a lock on it. I grabbed what I could from my room, which wasn't much and I high-tailed it out of there. I ran until I was too exhausted to move again. Sometime in the middle of the night, I came across a truck with a flatbed that was parked behind this garage. It had a large tarp in it and I figured I'd get some sleep before getting back on the road and getting out of Jersey."

"You slept outside in the back of a truck at fourteen?" Justine asked, shocked.

"I did and it was the best night of sleep that I'd had in years. Can you imagine that? Years? I got up just as daylight approached, grabbed my things and instead of continuing to run away, I went back to school. All day I looked around for my foster father to show up, but he never did. I showered in the gym and went to practice after school. I met a lot of cool guys and another guy from my high school team actually made it to professional football, too. He plays in Florida and we still stay in contact. Anyway, after practice, I didn't know what to do. I didn't have any money and still had only the three outfits to my name. I begged for money on the streets and got enough for a fast food meal. When I found myself sleepy, I ended up back at that same truck, climbed in and went to sleep. I thought no one knew I was there and that I would be safe as long as I got up early in the morning. I did that for a few nights and then one morning I woke up and standing there staring at me was Paul. He didn't look upset, pissed or angry, he just looked. He asked me why was I sleeping in the back of his truck. He said his wife had seen me a few times and finally sent him to check on me. I didn't say much other than I didn't have a place to live and that his truck was the only place to sleep that I could find that was close to my school. We talked for a bit and I felt comfortable. I didn't tell him about my foster family. That morning, I was about to head back to school after apologizing for sleeping in his truck when he invited me in to get something to eat and to shower. At first I didn't know his angle because I had trust issues, but when I met Minnie, she was the epitome of everyone's favorite grandmother. They had a daughter who was away at college and when I finished eating a meal of eggs, grits, toast and pancakes that Minnie made, I thought I had died and gone to heaven. They were nice and concerned about my well-being saying it wasn't safe to sleep outside and the weather was going to turn cold soon. Paul told me he was going to set up a cot for me in their basement and for me to come back after school if I still didn't have a place to go."

Justine exhaled and tears of joy pooled in her eyes.

"My goodness. Now, I love Paul and Minnie even more. They did that for you and they didn't have to," Justine said.

"Yes. They were truly my angels. For the next several months, that became my routine. Paul started giving me a lift to school on his way to work at an auto repair shop he owned. Then one day, social services came to the school and I thought all was lost. They did a home visit on me and my foster father told them I had run away months ago. I was only fourteen so they began looking for me and started at the school. When they found out I was still going to school every day, the counselor called me into his office. I told them what had happened and though they appreciated what Paul and Minnie had done by taking me in, they had to put me in a new foster home. Paul and Minnie tried to sign up to be my foster family, but there was a process they had to go through and until they did, I had to go. The good thing is I was placed in a group home and I was allowed to still spend time with Minnie and Paul. He showed me how to fix cars and they came to every single one of my games. Even though I no longer lived with them, Paul would get up early in the morning and drive to the group home to take me to school. Minnie would pack a lunch for him to bring to me and every so often new clothes for me to wear. At the end of the day, Paul would sometimes pick me up when I had a late practice so that I wasn't walking through the streets alone. That Christmas, I spent the day with them and that's when I finally met Andrea. I was nervous, not sure of her reaction, but Paul had told her all about me and when she met me, she called me her brother and said she always wanted a little brother. We were like brother and sister from day one."

Justine had to fan her face to keep tears from falling. She was overwhelmed by the thought of the guardian angels that were sent to protect the man she loved. She knew that his could have turned out a whole lot different.

"Remind me to get her an extra special Christmas present this year," Justine joked to lighten the mood a little. She felt like she'd succeeded when he let out a hearty laugh.

Kenrick already felt better finally telling her about his life.

"A few months later, I was getting up early on a Saturday morning to go help Minnie pull weeds in her garden and plant some flowers when I walked out of the door of the group home and sitting out front in his truck was Paul. I wasn't expecting him and when he said go grab my things, I thought he meant my backpack I often carried. He said that's not what he meant. He meant for me to grab all of my things because he and Minnie had been approved for me to live with them if I still wanted to. I turned to see the group home mother standing at the door and she said it was fine until the lady from social services came by to talk to me on Monday to be sure it's what I wanted to do. The rest, as they say, is history and I never looked back. They helped me finish high school, get into college and made sure I trained well for my career in football. I was able to get grants for college and Paul and Minnie helped and did more than any non-parent would ever do. I am who I am today because of them. Every time I looked out into the stands while I played college ball I saw them. When Andrea was home, she would make signs with my name on them and wear my jersey number. They were my real family," he declared.

"So, Paul owned an auto body shop back then. How did he come to own the three pool halls he now owns?" Justine asked.

"He's always wanted to own one. He would go play pool every Friday night and I would sit and keep Minnie company. We would play card games, board games and she'd help me with school work. She was an elementary school teacher. I had a great life with them and as soon as I signed my contract to play professional ball, the first thing I did was rebuild their home, making it bigger and brighter like Minnie should have and I bought Paul the buildings and built his pool halls. He has expanded each one to include a restaurant and the largest even has a supper club. It's something he's always wanted and I was able to make that happen. They did everything for me and because of them, I was able to know what love felt like. Andrea always wanted to go to Paris. I gave her a trip for a month in Paris and she met the love of her life and moved there. They turned my life around, but there is still a part of me that has been holding back from giving you all of me and I'm ashamed to say that I haven't always done the right thing by you," he admitted.

"What are you talking about? You have been my knight in shining armor from day one," she said.

"We have gone about our life sort of backwards, don't you think? Three kids and no wedding? How do you feel about that?" he asked.

"I feel that our love is on the path it's supposed to be on and everything happens in its own time. I love you and maybe our love isn't the status quo, but our love is deep and we love and raise our kids together in a loving environment. I will marry you whenever you feel you are ready and until then, we're going to live our lives our way, baby, and I don't want you to worry about me looking around every corner for an engagement ring. Let's love as we have been doing and when it's time, we'll both know. I am never going anywhere because I love you and you are good to me. I'm here forever, no matter what. How's that?" she answered smiling.

Before Kenrick could answer, Justine kissed him and he felt her passion for him in the kiss. He kissed her back fervently, leaving no doubt that he was on the same page as her when it came to their love. He feverishly fed from her mouth as she used her mouth to make love to his. As his body yearned for her and his hardness sought out her softness, he inhaled when she raised her body up above his and slid down slowly over his already hardened flesh.

"Thank you for letting me vent," Kenrick said on a whisper.

"Thank you for sharing with me. I will always be here and you can always tell me anything. Now, let me help clear your head of anything untoward," she said, moving her hips in a swirling motion, loving him.

Reaching down into the water, Kenrick cupped her luscious behind and helped guide her movements as she swirled her hips in a rhythm that drove him insane with need. He kissed the fullness of her bottom lip and traced the curve of her lips from one side to the other. He attempted to speak to let her know she was his everything.

"No words, just feel," Justine said. "Just feel, baby."

Kenrick did just that. He felt all of Justine as she made love to him. He held on to her hips as she gripped the sides of the tubs and gave him everything she had.

As they locked gazes, Kenrick knew he was a goner as his body tensed under her movements. She didn't rush because their love never needed to be hurried. The moment he felt the tingle that cascaded through is body, he knew he couldn't hold onto his restraint much longer and he wanted her with him. Aligning his hands on the edge of the tub alongside hers, he surged up into her body and they exploded together even as water sloshed over the edge and onto the floor.

As their bodies relaxed from the mutual eruption,

Kenrick wound his fingers through the long tresses of Justine's hair and pulled her mouth down on his for a kiss as powerful as the orgasm he'd just experienced.

"Forever with you I will always be. Thank you for loving me and always being there for me," Kenrick said.

"Forever and always," Justine responded and laid her head on his shoulder.

8 – Take a Knee

After leaving the gym, Kenrick was ready to do what his heart had been telling him for years. He was glad he asked his security detail to take the day off, giving him some time alone.

After the night he's spent with Justine in the tub where he poured his past out to her, he'd made love to her again once they reached the bed and that night, he'd slept better than he had in a long time. Josiah was right that he needed to share his past with Justine and finally let it go. His past should have died with his father, but he held on to it as if he needed to be punished every day or his past. He woke up the next morning and while letting her sleep a little late, he gathered the kids, got them dressed and made breakfast. When her parents joined him in the kitchen, they finished making breakfast together and talked about the upcoming Christmas holiday. Everyone was jovial and soon talk turned to his upcoming games. Once Justine joined them and he heated up her food, he took stock of the visual in front of him and was reminded how important family was.

Later that day, as her parents went out to visit friends, he and Justine sat in the family room with the kids huddled up with them under blankets as they pigged out on snack food and watch kid movies. That day, he realized how perfect his life was. No man could ask for more than the scene that was displayed that day.

Jazzy, who stayed in his arms the whole time, didn't want anyone else to hold her, but him. The boys laid on either side of them and for hours, that's what they did. They were a family and he knew at that moment, he needed to make it more permanent. He knew that if he proposed on Christmas, it wouldn't be as special as a long thought out and planned proposal event and for that he would need a little more time. He was now ready to put his plan in place.

Now with the new year coming in, it was time for newness all around. As he walked to his car, he pulled out his phone and called someone he knew could help him get what he needed. Who better to go to than the man who had all of the right connections.

"Diddy, I need your help!" he declared the minute he answered. He smiled, thankful for the friendship they'd developed over the past few years. Though he missed a lot of his big parties, they stayed in contact.

"What's up QB? Still killing the game I see!"

"Yeah, I'm doing a little something on the field. Listen, I need to connect with your jeweler to have a special engagement ring made for Justine. Can you help me with that?" he asked.

"You ready to make that move, huh? That's what I'm talking about! I have the perfect one for you. He will design whatever you need and he'll do it as fast as you want."

He listened and captured the number and to the advice to be sure and mention his name when he called. Kenrick thanked him and as soon as the call disconnected, he placed the call he knew would change his life.

He dialed and they talked for an hour, making plans for the jeweler to meet him in New York to show him some diamond samples. At the end of the call, Kenrick knew that the ring was taken care of and now, he needed something special put in place to pull off the engagement of the century. If he was able to do everything he'd been thinking about, it was going to take a lot of people and a lot of moving, coordinated parts. He placed a call to his brother.

"Josiah! Are you going to be in town for my next home game in two weeks?" he asked.

"Of course. This is the big playoff game and I wouldn't miss it. What's going on?" Josiah asked.

I want to propose to Justine and I want it to be big, very big. I'm going to need your help with my plan along with her mother and father."

"Really? That's exciting and it's about time!"

"It's way past time. I can't believe I waited this long."

"Bro, we both know what you were going through and it's understandable. You said you told Justine everything. She didn't hold anything against you, did she?"

Kenrick smiled thinking about Justine. She was the best and there were days when he felt like he didn't deserve someone as wonderful as her.

"No and she was loving and sympathetic and she remained the incredible woman I always knew she was. She couldn't believe that little boy is the same man she loves today."

"I'm sure once she heard your story, she expected that you would have turned out differently, harder, not as loving as you are. I told you, your past didn't have to be your future. I give you credit for not wanting to be anything like our father and for Paul and Minnie for coming in and saving you from yourself. They were able to show you that not every parent or parent figure would be like our father and your mother," Josiah said.

"I owe a lot to Paul, Minnie and Andrea. You know, she was an only child and she didn't have to accept me into their lives as if I was a family member, but she did. She treated me like the typical little brother. I wish she could be here for the engagement, but she was just here for Christmas and the game is in two weeks."

"Well, whatever you do, you can tape it or even stream it live for her. We can work that out. What do you have planned?" Josiah asked.

With extra excitement, Kenrick laid the plan out and hoped he wasn't going too far over the top.

~ ~

"Lane, you have a call on line two," the receptionist said.

Lane wasn't sure who would be calling her on her office line that the receptionist would answer. Most people she knew called her on her direct line at the courthouse where she clerked.

"Hello, this is Lane Geller," she said.

"Lane, it's Kenrick. How are you."

"Kenrick? Is everything okay? Is Justine okay?" she asked nervously.

"Everyone is fine. I'm sorry for calling you at work. I don't have your cell number and I didn't want to ask Justine for it."

"Are you sure everything is okay?"

Lane was caught off guard because she had never been called by Kenrick directly before. She and her husband, Omar, were friends with Kenrick and Justine and had been for years. They hung out often as a couple and she and Omar enjoyed the first class treatment they received whenever they attended one of his football games. Never had she been called by Kenrick, which led her to believe something was wrong.

"Lane, all is fine. I'm calling because I'm going to propose to Justine and I want to be sure you and Omar will be there. I may need your help with a few things, especially with keeping things a secret from her."

"What!" Lane shouted in the phone causing him to

hold his cell away from his ear.

"Seriously, Lane?" he laughed.

"What? This is huge and I'm happy for you. Congratulations and I'm here to do anything you need me to do. You already know Omar and I will be there for the event. What do you need me to do?" she asked.

"Well, I know you and Justine have a lot of friends in common and I want them in attendance when I propose. I'm hoping to do something big at the stadium and if I can pull it off, everyone will need tickets to get in, which is why I need a head count. Also, the girlfriends and wives of the players will be there and I want to be sure I have someone coordinating with them. Can you do that?" he asked.

"Of course. Anything for you and Justine. This is the best news ever!" Lanc said.

"It's going to be a pretty big proposal."

"Do you have the ring?" she asked.

"I just made the call about that. I have a jeweler flying in this week."

"Wait, you're flying a jeweler in? This is major. Justine is going to so surprised. She deserves it, you know."

"Justine deserves this and much more, trust me, I know that. I've always known. Now, get a pen and let me give you some numbers in order to reach the wives and girlfriends organization. Remember when you reach out to your friends, make it clear that no one can tell Justine anything and to not act crazy if they see or talk to her. She deserves this big day in her honor and I want to do it right," Kenrick said.

"I got it covered."

Getting in his car, Kenrick gave her full instructions and excitement flowed through him at what was going to happen. He couldn't wait to be married to Justine.

After the call ended, he had one last call to make for the day. He would reach out to his coach when he got to practice because he needed him to pull a few strings. For now, he had a bigger call to make.

9 – Take a Knee

Kenrick rushed through the airport the moment his plane touched down in Dallas, Texas. Thankfully, he didn't have to go far to connect with Justine's father, allowing him to get back on his return flight in a few hours.

After getting permission to leave right after his last practice of the day, he'd called Justine's father and asked if they could talk. He smiled at the surprised tone of his voice when he announced he wanted to talk in person and would be flying into Dallas for a quick chat. After Prentiss asked him if Justine and the kids were okay, he reassured him that they were and stated that he wanted to have a sit down with him about something personal. They agreed to meet at a restaurant close to the airport.

With Cesar leading the way, he followed him out of the airport and into the waiting truck that Cesar had secured from the plane.

"Big changes are coming, Cesar," he said after he was settled in the back seat. Cesar took the seat next to the driver.

"All for the good of things," Cesar said.

Kenrick smiled the whole ride to the restaurant, which didn't take long since it was only eight blocks from the exit of the airport. He hopped out as soon as they pulled up to the restaurant. Cesar got out to open the back door and then got back in to wait with the driver. The chat between Kenrick and Justine's father was a private one, he knew. They needed to speak alone.

"I shouldn't be long and I know we have a flight to catch. I'll make this quick," Kenrick said as he turned and headed inside. He looked around and spotted Justine's father sitting in the back in a booth and he headed in his direction.

"Mister Banks," he said as Prentiss stood to greet him.

"It's good to see you, Kenrick."

They sat down across from each other.

"It's good to be seen and thanks for agreeing to meet with me at the last minute like this. I know it was a surprise and as I stated, Justine and the kids are fine and nothing is wrong. In fact, everything is right. Let me start by saying thank you for the talk we had back in November. As I said back then, I understood what you were saying as far as you looking out for your daughter. I have Jazzy now and during a conversation with my brother, he asked me how I would feel if Jazzy were a young woman coming home to tell me she was in love and instead of him marrying her and doing the right thing, she starts popping out his babies. Though they may have some kind of commitment, it wouldn't be the kind of commitment a father would want for his daughter and I can respect that."

Prentiss smiled at him.

"I know you love my daughter and I've never, ever questioned that. I'm glad you understood what I was trying to say. Justine is my baby and I want the best for her. I know that's you, but I also know it needs to be all of you and that, again, is speaking as her father," Prentiss said.

"That's why I'm here today, sir. I don't want to make a lot of excuses about why I did or didn't do something, but my life was a lot different than Justine's. I won't go into a lot of detail right now, but one day, I hope to be able to sit down with you and your wife and tell you more about where I came from and what my life was like. What I will say now is that I had a terrible life until around the age of fourteen when Paul and Minnie took me in and showed me what it felt like to be loved even though I wasn't their son by birth. They were better parents to me than my parents ever were and because of the parents I had as a child, I had trust issues. I know Justine loves me and she always has, but my internal struggles held me back from making that final commitment because I never knew what real commitment was. I was afraid of it because I never saw it as a child, not until I met Paul and Minnie. I didn't even know my brother until four years ago after I hired a private eye to look for him and my other siblings."

Prentiss perked up.

"You have other siblings besides Josiah?" he asked.

"Yes. Josiah is the oldest by a few years. We have the same father but different mothers. We also have a sister who is younger than me and two other siblings, all by my father, but again separate mothers. It's a long, crazy story and I promise, one day, I will fill you in on all of the sordid details of my youth. I'm here today for a special reason. I love Justine, Jazzy, Erick and Ricky more than my own life and I can't imagine not having them. They are what make me who I am. I learned to love when I met Justine and I learned to love deeper with the birth of our children. The only thing I'm sorry for is the order in which we've done things," he declared.

Kenrick reached into his pocket and pulled out a black velvet box with a ribbon made of real gold tied around it. He placed it on the table between them.

"Oh my," Prentiss said, seeing the significance of the meeting.

"I love your daughter and I flew all this way to Dallas to ask you for her hand in marriage. I promise you I will love, honor and cherish her for the rest of my life and I do plan to live the rest of my life with her. This is something I should have done eight years ago, before Ricky was born and I'm hoping you'll forgive me for not doing it then and accept me for doing it now."

Kenrick reached over and opened the box to a stunning twenty carat, Bulgari engagement ring, more exquisite than anything he'd ever seen himself. When the jeweler delivered it in person, he couldn't believe how magnificent the ring was. It was well worth the four million dollars he'd paid for it. He saw her father's eyes practically pop out of his head when he saw it.

"That's a remarkable ring. It sure is a beauty. How much security would Justine have to walk around with for protection?" Prentiss said and smiled.

"Well, sir, this is the first of three rings. I won't mind if she wants to wear this one and of course she will always have her protection detail when she's out and not with me. I have three other rings, smaller than this one that she can change into depending on what she's doing and what she feels comfortable wearing out."

Prentiss picked up the ring and turned it around to really get a good look at it.

"I've never seen anything more beautiful than this," he raved. "Nothing would give me greater pleasure than to have you as my son-in-law. You are perfect for my daughter and I love seeing you with your kids. I don't know much about your life as a child , but I know you as a man and there is none greater than you. You certainly have my blessing and I speak for my wife when I say we welcome you into this family with open arms. Justine is going to love this. When do you plan on proposing?" Prentiss asked.

"Well, that's where you come in. I have something big set up and I'm going to need your help. I have a home game in a week and I'm hoping you and your wife could make it to New Jersey for it."

"Of course, we can. This is the playoff game and we were hoping to fly in for it."

"That's great. I'll have a flight lined up for you and of course, you can stay at the house. That wing is pretty much yours all the time anyway," Kenrick laughed.

"You're not just good to Justine, you're good to us."

"You and your wife make it easy, trust me on that. Now, I need our help with something else. I don't have a lot of family, but I know Justine does and I want you to see how many of them can make it to Jersey for the game. I'll have tickets and jerseys for everyone and I'm covering everyone's airfare and hotel for two nights. I need to know who and how many and I'll have my assistant make all of the arrangements. I'll give him your number and the two of you can get this ball rolling. I have something big planned for the proposal and I want her surrounded by those who love her and those she loves. I have a lot of people working on this and I'll share more with you in a few days. I'm waiting on a call about the biggest part of my plan and as long as that's in place, we are good to go. Right now, I have to catch a flight back to New Jersey and get home to my family. We are having a family movie night tonight and it's Disney until the kids fall asleep. Are you in?" he asked.

Prentiss smiled widely.

"I'm all in, son."

"Okay, here's what I'll need," Kenrick said.

For the next twenty minutes, he shared as much as he could about his plans and how he thought Prentiss should handle getting their family members to New Jersey without anyone slipping up and saying anything to Justine. He wanted her to be surprised. Game day was going to be a good day!

As he and Prentiss stood to leave, Kenrick turned and hugged him.

"Thank you for trusting me with your daughter. I promise, you will never regret doing so," he said.

Prentiss clapped him on the back and tried to hold back tears. He couldn't ask for a better man for his only daughter.

~~

"How did it go?" Cesar asked the minute Kenrick entered the truck.

"Everything went fine. I'm glad I'm finally doing this. I know her father had his concerns, but there was never anything to be concerned about. Justine always has been and always will be the love of my life."

"You definitely lucked out with her. Any man would be blessed to have a woman like Justine in his corner," Cesar said.

"That he would. How much time do we have before the flight?" he asked.

"By the time we get back to the airport, we'll have an hour which will be ate up with boarding and take off preparations."

"Good because I'm ready to get back to my family," Kenrick said. He was about to continue when his cell rang. Thinking it was probably Justine wondering what time he would be coming home, he answered.

"Hey, baby," he said without looking to see who was calling.

"Hi, darling!" his coach said and then laughed out loud.

"Coach?" Kenrick asked.

"Yeah."

Kenrick laughed himself.

"Sorry about that. I thought you were Justine."

"Hey, I needed that laugh. Listen, I'm calling to let you know that everything is a go for you on game day. I spoke with the owners and they love the idea and support you. The only thing that has to be done is details have to be worked out with the stadium staff on what you'll need for that day. As long as everything is completed at least two hours before game time, you're good. It's a night game and I told them you were asking for early afternoon time. Is that still the case?" he asked.

"Yes, it is. What about the tickets I'll need for all the guests?" Kenrick asked.

After getting the names from Lane all he had to do was wait on Justine's father to give him a head count and he would know how many tickets he would need. To be sure, he asked for two hundred, most of stadium seating while others would be in the skybox he asked to use for the day. Being the team quarterback, he was often catered to, though he didn't take advantage of it often. This time, he would. He needed everything to play out the way he'd been dreaming about.

"I've already secured you two hundred seats and if you need more, let me know. You still have your usual twenty comped tickets. You'll also have two skyboxes for that day. I'll leave all of the rest of the planning to you."

"Sounds good coach. I appreciate your help. I have Justine's best friend, Lane, working with the stadium staff for catering and other details."

"Great. I'll have the tickets delivered to your assistant by tomorrow. I hope I'm invited to the proposal. Sounds like it's going to be huge!" Coach Mason said.

"Of course. I'm expecting the entire team. I asked the guys at practice the other night and everyone was glad to be a part."

"I'm happy for you and Justine. You deserve all the happiness in the world."

"Thanks, Coach. I now believe that too," Kenrick said.

10 – Take a Knee

Kenrick burst through the front door of his house and within seconds, he heard the sound of two pair of feet running to greet him. He looked up as his pride and joy, Erick and Ricky bound down the stairs toward him. He stooped and picked them up into his arms as they leaped.

"Daddy!" Ricky exclaimed.

"Hey, boys! Where's mommy and Jazzy?" he asked.

"Upstairs. Mommy is packing a bag for you and Jazzy is asleep as usual," Ricky said. "We're going to your game."

"I heard and I'm excited. I love when I look out and see you cheering for me. Have you been practicing your cheer?" he asked Erick.

"Yes. Ricky has been practicing with me," Erick replied.

"Good. I want to hear big, loud cheers from both of

you."

"Grandma and grandpa are here, too. Mommy was surprised they were here. She said she didn't know they were going to your game, too," Ricky said.

Kenrick smiled knowing that he knew why they were in town for the game. They went to a few of his games throughout the year, but this one was a special game and he was ready for it. A few more days and their lives were going to change.

"That's good," Kenrick chatted as they walked up the long winding staircase to the upper level.

"Mommy! Daddy's home!" Ricky chimed, running ahead of him.

"Hey, babe!" Justine cheered as he walked into the bedroom. "Ricky, I told you and Erick to get ready for your baths or no one is going to the game in two days."

They laughed when Erick and Ricky shot by them and ran into their own bedroom.

"I guess that means they plan to go to the game," Kenrick said as he leaned down and kissed Justine sweetly on the lips.

"I guess so. I wasn't expecting you this early. I thought you would fly through here later, grab your clothes and run back out."

Kenrick looked at the bed and at the clothes and other items she'd been laying out for him.

"I know. I had a couple of meetings after the team practice today."

Are you home for long or headed to the hotel?" she asked.

"I'm home long enough to kiss my babies, grab something to eat and that's pretty much it. Your parents are here?" he asked.

"Yes. I was surprised to see them. My mom didn't mention they were coming in for the game when I talked to her last week. I'm glad they're here. They were a great help with the kids today. My dad took the boys out and mom helped with Jazzy while I got some shopping done. The new jerseys for the kids came in, including a new one for Jazzy. With those fat little arms she has, the shirt we had for her is already too small."

Kenrick laughed. He loved his six-month-old butterball.

"Speaking of the jerseys, can you have everyone dressed and at the stadium a little early for the game?" he asked.

"How early?"

"Well, there will be some on-field activities, relays and things that the kids can take part in before the big playoff game. I want Erick and Ricky to take part. Luckily, it looks like the weather will cooperate and it won't be as cold as it has been lately. For the game, I want you to watch from the skybox though, especially with Jazzy. Do we have new jerseys for your parents?" he asked.

"Yes, we have tons. They can pick through and get ones that are in their size."

"So, you're all set for Sunday. It's going to be a good day," Kenrick said. What he didn't say was that it was going to be a good day for more reasons than just the game.

Thanks to the owners, he had a big day planned before the game even gets started. The key to it all was to have Justine at the stadium early.

"You still didn't say what time you wanted us at the stadium? I need to be sure the car is here on time," Justine said.

"Don't worry about that. I'll have special transportation since your parents are here, that'll get all of you to the stadium by two."

"For a game that starts at seven?" Justine asked.

"Yes, remember the fun activities. Bring Hannah with you. She can help you with Jazzy while you help with the boys. I'll be in the locker room most of the time. Is that cool?" he asked.

"Of course. Whatever time you need us there, we will be there."

Kenrick pulled her into his arms and pushed the door to close quietly behind them.

"What are you doing, Kenrick?" Justine said, having an idea of his intentions. She went into his arms as he pulled her close.

"I'm loving on my woman with the few seconds we'll have before either our sons come barging in or our daughter wakes up and you know how her timing is. I'm starting to believe she has a camera in our bedroom and the moment she sees action is about to take place, she screams and interrupts us," he joked.

Kenrick leaned down and nuzzled her neck, kissing around from one side to the other. Before she could protest knowing the kids were in their room, he untied the belt around her silk robe and inhaled her scent as his eyes settled on her nakedness underneath.

"Damn! You're naked underneath this robe and I've been wasting my time talking?" he quipped.

"Well, if I knew you were going to come home in an amorous mood, I would have sent the boys to the wing where your parents are," she said.

"Where's Hanna?" he asked.

"Doing Jazzy's laundry. You know hers has to be done separate from everyone else's."

"Call her and have her keep an eye on the boys for about fifteen minutes and then you can give them their baths," he said with a sexy undertone.

"Okay, I can do that, but for future reference, let's go with thirty minutes and not fifteen. Not that you can't get the job done in fifteen minutes, I prefer a quickie that's at least thirty minutes. Get naked, lover boy and I'll get the Hannah."

"You don't have to tell me twice to get ready for a good time," Kenrick said and raced to the bathroom to grab a quick shower. This was his life and he wouldn't change it for anything.

~~

Paul walked into his house and found his wife Minnie sitting at their kitchen table smiling.

"Honey, what's got you in such a smiling mood?" he asked, sitting down across from her. He'd been gone all day checking on each of the pool halls before finally making his way back home. Looking over at her, he couldn't help but appreciate how perfect his life was.

"Well, I'm thinking about Kenrick and Justine. I'm happy he's going to propose to her. I've been concerned about him for a long time," Minnie said.

"I know, so have I. He's doing good."

"He is. He's a lot different than that boy we took in many years ago. Since that day, I have been thankful that he was in our lives. When we weren't blessed with more children after Andrea, I thought that would be it and I was happy with her. Then along comes Kenrick, the son we prayed for. He didn't come the traditional way, but he turned into ours. I'm proud of the man he is."

"He has made us proud. I wasn't sure what he would be like after what he'd been through. My heart ached for him after the social worker told us what his life had been like. No child should live like that. I'm glad you saw him in the back of my truck that morning. There's no telling what would have happened to him out in those streets," Paul said.

"Now, look at him today. He's a professional ball player, living a good life and has Justine and three beautiful children. I'm excited about them getting married."

"It's nice that he continues to include us in every aspect of their lives. I don't know that I was expecting that. When we took him in, I wanted to be sure he had the knowledge and skills to take care of himself and the compassion needed to love, something we know he never received before coming to live with us. I'm proud to call him son, even if he isn't my son," Paul said.

"Kenrick is your son in every way that matters and I'm not surprised he still calls us mom and pop. We poured love into him, giving him an extra heaping of it because he needed it. To see him with his own family brings me joy," Minnie expressed.

"Well, in two more days, he'll take a step that you and I have been praying he would take for some years now. I'm believing this is a result of him finally letting go of that messy childhood and walking into a future where the slate has been wiped clean."

"I'm with you. He stopped by early today and brought us new jerseys to wear to the game. He's one remarkable young man," Minnie said.

"Yes he is and he's our son," Paul exclaimed.

11 – Take a Knee

"Mom, can you help me get the boys ready? Hannah has Jazzy and is just about finished getting her ready. I don't want to be late and the limousine Kenrick sent is already in the driveway," Justine said rushing around.

"The boys aren't dressed yet?" her mother said, rushing into the bedroom.

"They've been too busy playing around. I just got myself dressed and now I need to wrangle them up. Can you help?" she asked. She was about to add more when she saw her mother turn around and head to the boys' bedroom. She knew she asked the right person to help her. The boys would straighten up now.

She smiled as she heard her mother quiet them down with the threat of staying home. When there was silence, she knew they were finally getting dressed and for that, she was thankful. It wasn't easy handling three kids, even with her nanny, Hannah around to help out. She didn't want to be late after Kenrick pleaded with her to let the boys participate in whatever was happening at the stadium before tonight's playoff game. He was specific about when he wanted them to arrive.

"They're ready!" her mother chimed from the other room.

"Good. Thanks, mom." Justine walked across the hall to Jazzy's room just as Hannah came out with her little bundle in her arms wiggling around.

"I think she wants you. She could hear you talking and I think she was looking for you," Hannah said.

Justine gathered Jazzy in her arms.

"Can you grab the bag I put together for her and meet us downstairs? Don't forget to put your jersey on," she said, noticing Hannah hadn't put hers on yet. "You're part of this family," she said sweetly. She never wanted Hannah to see herself only as someone who they employed. It was important that she felt like part of the family.

Tonight's game was a special one because it was the playoff game. The expectation was that he and his team would win tonight and she knew that he loved knowing they were somewhere in the stadium supporting him.

Before having Jazmine, she would sit in the section with other player's girlfriends and wives, but with her still being so young, she was going to watch the game from the warmth and comfort of the skybox, while her father and Kenrick's brother watched the game from the sidelines with Erick and Ricky. The boys loved the hustle and comradery that took place amongst the team on the sideline.

Finally making it downstairs, she was surprised to see her boys calm, ready to go and standing at the door. He father had left hours earlier telling them that Kenrick had asked him to help with some of the prep for the activities. She loved the close relationship Kenrick had developed with her father, especially after hearing what his life was like as a child.

That night after making love, she'd stayed up and watched him sleep, thinking of the torture he must have gone through as a child. She looked to the scars on his upper arms and rubbed them softly with her fingers. She knew those were the scars that his father had inflicted on him using lighted cigarettes. She then looked down at his legs and remembered the long mark that never healed from the buckle of the belt his father had used to beat him with. She cried softly, not wanting to wake him, knowing the pain he must have been in. Through all of that, she was blessed that he had turned out to be the loving, caring man that he was and she would do anything for his happiness. Thanks to the love and support he received from Paul, Minnie and their daughter Andrea, Kenrick was able to make it through that turmoil and thrive. She was living a blessed life with the love of her life and nothing could make her happier.

"You ready to go?" she said to Erick and Ricky who nodded their heads incessantly.

"We're all ready," her mother said coming down the steps followed by Hannah.

"I was wondering what was taking you so long," she

said.

"We were getting things straight upstairs," her mother said.

While she wrapped the baby up and put her in her covered car seat, Justine watched as her mother and Hannah got the boys coats on and they all headed toward the waiting limousine.

"We're right on schedule," Justine said checking the time.

"You know I wasn't going to allow us to be late. It's going to be a lot of fun," her mother said.

What Justine didn't see was the sly look her mother and Hannah exchanged. She was the only one who didn't know what the day would entail.

~ ~

Kenrick paced around the locker room like a man waiting outside of the birthing room at a hospital.

"Kenrick, you're going to wear a hole in the floor. Sit down, dude," Josiah said.

"Do you know what today is?" Kenrick asked, nervously.

"I sure do and I'm just as excited as you are. Justine is a beautiful woman and she's going to make a gorgeous bride and an incredible wife and partner for life for you. This plan you have in place is going to be the talk of the town for years to come. I can't believe you actually pulled this off."

"Well, I haven't pulled it off yet, but thanks to the owners and the staff here at the stadium, we are ready. Did you see all of Justine's family and friends that are here? We have to have them all secluded in a private room. I don't want her running into any of them," Kenrick boomed.

"I saw the crowd. Looked like fifty or so members of her family," Josiah stated.

"I'm glad they're here."

Josiah looked at Kenrick and knew what he was thinking.

"You have family here today, too. I'm here, my wife and kids are here. Paul and Minnie are here. Your friends from the neighborhood where you grew up living with Paul and Minnie are here today and you know the team is with you. From what I hear, they are just as excited as you are. One player told me that he wouldn't miss it for anything. He loves the leadership role you've taken with the team and just like they support you each time the team took a knee for the cause, they support you in this too. They wanted to be sure you had friends around to hold you up today," Josiah reminded him. Kenrick needed to know that he had a lot of support.

Kenrick smiled gleefully. It wasn't until he started making plans for today's proposal that he realized how many friends he had. He spent a lot of time going back to the old neighborhood where Paul and Minnie still lived and hanging with friends he'd had for many years. They spent a lot of time together during his off-season time and anytime he needed them, they were there.

Paul and Minnie never missed any of his games or anything else he was involved in. Whenever their daughter Andrea was in town, they were as close as any two siblings could be even though they weren't sibling by blood. She couldn't make it to the game, but she was planning on coming whenever they had the wedding. Paul and Minnie would represent for all three of them.

He loved being able to go into town to the house where they took him in, though he'd had it rebuilt a few years back. He offered to buy or build them a brand new house anywhere they wanted, but they opted to stay where they were and were grateful that he wanted to refurbish their current house, buying the land next to them to expand the size of the house. They were his family, along with Josiah and his family and he was lucky to have them stand with him today.

"I'm thankful for all of you, especially you. I'm glad that private eye found you. Now, if he could find the rest of our siblings, my world would be complete," Kenrick remarked.

"Anything else from him?" Josiah asked, hoping to change the subject, allowing Kenrick to relax a little. Though the rest of the family and the team would be in his jersey for the proposal, he was dressed in a black and gray tuxedo, making the moment special.

"I got a message from him earlier today, actually. He said he had some news for us and he'd like to talk to you and I tomorrow. I told him I would check to be sure that worked for you and give him a call later. I hope what he has is good news," Kenrick said. He'd been worried that the others would never be found. He knew that contact had been made with their sister who was a year younger than him. They were waiting on word that she was interested in meeting them. He asked that the private investigator not reveal who he was by name, so that their sister would want to meet them and not just Kenrick Wilson, professional multi-million-dollar football player.

"Maybe our sister is ready to meet us. What about the younger two?" Josiah asked.

"I'm hoping he has some news on them. The only thing he could find the last time we talked about a month ago was that they were somewhere in the foster care system. We'll see tomorrow. I'll call him later tonight after the game. Are Justine and the kids here yet?" he asked, jumping back into the purpose for the day.

"Her father just sent me a text that they were down on the field. Hannah has Jazzy up in the skybox where it's warmer, but she would bring her down right before you came out. We have to let him know when we're ready. Your mother is on the field with Justine helping with the boys. Her family is ready and they'll come out behind you as you enter the field from the tunnel. Are you ready?" Josiah queried.

"I've been ready for this. Let's do it," Kenrick commented.

Josiah got on his phone and got everyone in place.

Kenrick checked his pocket for the ring box and picked up the dozen white roses that were laying on the bench.

"Everyone's ready. The team, her family, Paul and

Minnie and your friends are all in the tunnel waiting for you. Lane is getting everyone in place. That little lady is a pistol, barking out orders," he laughed.

Kenrick laughed, needing to relax with his nerves going crazy.

"She's on her way to being a lawyer, so that fits her personality. She was vital in pulling all of this off."

"Where's my baby girl," he asked, making sure he didn't go out until all of his kids were on the field.

"Hannah is bringing Jazzy down to the field after getting her all bundled up and the staff is ready for your cue. Let's do this, bro," Josiah said.

Kenrick nodded and followed his brother out of the locker room and toward his destiny.

12 – Take a Knee

"When do the activities for the boys start?" Justine asked her father.

"Any minute now," he responded.

"I see all of the other player's kids out here, but I don't see any of the team players. I thought they were apart of all of this? Kenrick said he would be here for a little bit to participate with the boys for some of it. I've called his cell a few times and he hasn't answered. I guess he's already put his phone away," Justine bemoaned. She was hoping the boys would have him with them as they played on the field. She knew how much it would mean to them.

"Justine, what's wrong? Why are you so antsy?" her mother said.

"I'm not. I'm not down here on the field too often and it's overwhelming. I think I'm nervous about the game tonight. Everyone is counting on Kenrick. I know he's had a winning season all along, but I don't want all the pressure on him. We're also playing against a team that doesn't support players taking a knee and you know Kenrick will lead the team in doing that tonight. I don't want to hear him get booed for doing so."

Justine was happy that the fans of the team supported them and a lot even took a knee in the stands. It was a lot of pressure for Kenrick to walk around with since a lot of the team looked to him as their leader. Her concern, as always, was for him.

"Justine, you can't control everyone's reactions to the team taking a knee. You know Kenrick and his reasons for supporting that movement. He may not have been mistreated as he goes about his life, but he has had some pain in his life that makes him sympathetic to the cause. All we can do is support him and let him know that we are behind him one hundred percent," her mother said.

"I know. He finally shared his life as a child with me and all I can say is he is blessed to be alive today. I have and always will support him, no matter what. He's been through so much and I don't want to see him disappointed or hurt."

"Kenrick will be fine," her mother opined.

"Justine Victoria Banks, can you hear me?"

Justine looked around to see where the summoning of her name had come from. It sounded like she could hear her name being called out over the loud speakers throughout the stadium.

"What was that? It sounded like Kenrick," she mumbled to her mother.

"Justine Victoria Banks, love of my life, are you

there?" the booming voice said again.

This time she knew it was Kenrick's voice. Her heart raced as she looked around to see if anyone else was hearing her name being called. She wasn't the only one who heard it as all eyes turned to her. There were no fans in the seats yet, only a few stadium employees walking about amongst the seats. She looked around the field and saw the players' wives and girlfriends turn toward her, smile and wave as they held on to their kids.

"I heard him that time and so did everyone else," she uttered.

"Look," her mother said and pointed.

Justine followed her mother's pointed finger and looked toward the large jumbotron where her image appeared larger than life. There was a camera someplace in the stadium and it was being pointed at her. She looked to her mother and father who both smiled at her like they knew the worlds most guarded secret. When she turned, she saw Hannah walk up behind her with Jazzy asleep and all bundled up in her arms. When she reached for Jazzy, her mother turned her attention back to the large screen and then to the entrance to the tunnel where Kenrick and his team usually entered the field during a game.

"Justine, baby!" she heard loudly. This time when she looked, she saw Kenrick walking out of the tunnel, not dressed in his uniform, but dressed in a black tuxedo looking like he was on his way to a black-tie affair. In his arms was a large bouquet of white roses, her favorite flower and her color. What surprised her most was behind and surrounding him as he made his way over to her was the entire football team, Kenrick's family and friends and most shocking was her family and friends being led by Lane. She also saw that every single person had on his jersey, except for the team players. Looking closer, she saw that they each had one single white rose in their hand.

"What's happening?" she said softly as her heart beat sped up. She looked over at her mother who already had tears rolling down her cheeks. Looking down at her boys, as if they were schooled on what to do, she saw them reach up and grabbed her hand on either side of her. Hannah moved in closer with Jazzy and her father leaned over to whisper in her ear.

"This is your day," he declared.

After looking up at him, she turned her attention back to Kenrick just as he approached her.

"Hi, baby," he gushed with pride coming up to her as she stood on the sideline.

Justine looked around nervously realizing she was the only one who didn't know what was going on.

"Kenrick, what is all this?" she said as everyone gathered around. She looked up at over one hundred members of her family and friends who were waving at her. Lane walked over and stood with her with tears running down her face.

"This is for you," he said.

"My family is all here," she uttered with disbelief.

"Yes, they are because they love you and so do I.

Today we have your family and friends, my family and friends, the team and their families here to stand with us before we play one of the biggest games of my career. Before that takes place, I wanted them to share in another big event today."

"Baby, what is going on?" Justine asked again as she began to shake nervously. She wasn't use to having a spotlight on her and all eyes on her and in the back of her mind, she began to get a clue. She had an idea of what was about to happen and she was overwhelmed with the amount of love she had for him. She never thought that anything could make her love him more, but he is showing her differently.

"Well, when we met nine years ago when I was twenty-one, I wasn't a whole man at that time. As I recently shared with you, I had a childhood that I wouldn't wish on an enemy and that childhood impacted me as an adult. I was battered, bruised, abused and unloved as a child. It wasn't until I turned fifteen after living with Paul and Minnie for almost a year that I allowed myself to believe that love actually existed and they taught me that. The little I did know, I wanted to give to you. Back then, I don't think I did it the right way, but you stuck it out with me. I didn't know back then that I would be playing professional ball, but you wanted me anyway. You were in New York going to college and I was hanging out in the city with some friends and in the middle of Times Square, I met the love of my life. I'm thankful that you gave me a chance, though I wasn't always the best boyfriend. Nine years later, we have three beautiful children and a fairytale life that some people only dream of. You've been caring, patient, dedicated, devoted, loving, kind, compassionate, understanding and you never judged. You've supported me and loved me, sacrificing some dreams I know you had for your own life to have and raise our family and take care of our home life, a place I can always come back to after being on the road. Our home is filled with love and wherever I go, I carry you and that love with me. Today, I want to bring that love here to you on this field where you have helped me make my dreams come true."

Kenrick felt more relaxed than he ever has because he was speaking from his heart. He found it easy to do as he looked into her beautiful eyes as he spoke. Today, he would take a knee for the most important reason in his life.

Justine was too overwhelmed to speak as pools of tears filled her eyes and fell down over her cheeks. She had more love for Kenrick than she ever had. He was never one to pour his heart out in public, but here he was laying it all on the line. She kept her eyes on him as he handed the flowers to Josiah and as he did at the start of each one of his football games, Kenrick got down on one knee. When he did, the entire team followed suit and took a knee with him.

"Baby!" was all she was able to get out before she began to cry harder. She felt so much joy, she could barely contain it. No one spoke and there was no sound in the stadium as Kenrick reached into his pocket and withdrew a black velvet box.

"Justine, you've supported me every time I took a knee at the start of my games to remain in solidarity with other players and other people across this country who wanted to send a message that we, together want to see a change. Today, I'm taking a knee, right now, to send a message that you are the love of my life and before I take a knee again for any other cause, I'm taking it for the most important cause and that is to make our family whole. I'm taking a knee because you are the woman of my dreams. I'm taking a knee because you complete me. I'm taking a knee because without you and our children, I would be nothing. I'm taking a knee because I love you so much and that love grows more and more each day. Today, as I take a knee, I'd like to ask you Justine Victoria Banks, if you would do me the honor of becoming my wife."

He did it, Kenrick thought. He overcame his insecurities and did what should have been done years ago. He took a knee for the woman who was his world.

Justine was crying so hard, she could barely speak. She tried to rub the tears from her eyes in order to focus, but through the happiness of everything that was happening, she couldn't wipe them away fast enough. She no longer cared about tears. Kneeling before her was the man who had made every dream she'd had in life come true. She was happier than any woman could ever be because she had the devoted love of an incredible man. For her, he was taking a knee and she loved him more and more with every passing second.

"Yes, baby! Yes!" she screamed and went into his arms as he stood to his full height. She held on tight for what seemed an eternity, not wanting to let go. She always knew Kenrick loved her and she was patient enough to allow him to find his way without any pressure from her. After they talked, she understood the hurdles in his personality that she often had to look the other way on because she knew deep down, he was the most incredible man she'd ever met. Nothing warmed her heart more than to see him with his children giving them the kind of love he needed, but didn't have as a child. She now understood his desire to have children early. She would have a million more because she knew he would love all of them equally.

Leaning back, she accepted the kiss Kenrick leaned down to place on her lips. It wasn't a quick peck, but a deep, passionate kiss. She received his kiss and gave as good as he was giving to her as she reached up and held on to his broad shoulders to keep from collapsing from the impact of it all. Around them, everyone clapped and cheered. Stepping back from her, she watched as Kenrick opened the ring box and took out a ring with a diamond in it, a size she never knew existed.

"Kenrick!" was all she could get out.

"I love you, baby," he said as he slid the large diamond on her finger.

Justine looked at the ring and then at her family and friends as one by one, they each laid their one white rose at her feet. The scene was one out of a romantic movie and a visual she would never, ever forget.

"I love you," Justine said looking up into Kenrick's eyes. He turned them so that they could see the large screen as fireworks shot off across it. That was followed by their favorite song being played over the speakers, "There's Nothing Better Than Love" by Luther Vandross and Gregory Hines.

Justine held on to Kenrick as Hannah handed Jazzy to him while Erick and Ricky came back up to hold on to her hands. As family gathered around them, pictures of her life with Kenrick flashed on the screen. Her heart warmed knowing the hurt of Kenrick's past would no longer hold any part of him hostage. They were in it for love.

13 – Take a Knee

Justine stretched in the king-sized bed after making love with Kenrick for the second time. They not only celebrated being engaged, but they celebrated his team's win at the playoff game.

After the on-field proposal, followed by many, many pictures being taken with all of their family and friends around, they then prepared for a little fun for the player's kids on the field while she retreated to the skybox with family. While they were on the field, the skybox had been set up with platters of delicious food and drinks and a large cake celebrating her and Kenrick's engagement. She spent the rest of the evening throughout the game reveling in the events of the day. She didn't know how Kenrick pulled it all off, but he'd arranged for sixty members of her family to fly in from various cities around the country all without her knowing anything about hit.

Lane, she found out, had been responsible for having a lot of her friends there and it was good to celebrate with them all. She and Lane shared a non-spoken look, knowing her dream of having Lane stand with her on her wedding day was going to come true. She later found out that her father had a hand in the planning, which excited her.

After their winning game and the team went out to celebrate, Kenrick opted to spend his evening with her and their kids. Instead of going back to their house in Alpine, they traveled to New York City to stay in the five bedroom condo they owned. They didn't want the kids far away, so when their parents went back to stay at the house in Alpine until they flew back home in a few days, they brought the kids with them, along with Hannah.

Somewhere throughout the morning, Hannah, who had known about the engagement, had packed a bag for each of the kids with enough clothes for a week. With the help of her mother, she had also packed clothes for her and Kenrick so that they wouldn't have to go to the house for anything. Instead, the plan was for their family to spend a week in the city as other teams vied for a spot in the playoffs. They were looking forward to spending some quality time together.

When they arrived at the condo, with the late hour, the boys were already fast asleep and had to be carried up to the condo. Once there, they were put in their beds where she was sure they would sleep through the night. It had been an exciting day for them.

Jazmine had been fed around midnight and if she woke in the night, Hannah would feed her a bottle, change her and put her back down. The night was going to belong to her and Kenrick.

"The way you're stretching, you're making me think I didn't love you hard enough to knock you out for the night," Kenrick joked.

Justine moved over and slid into Kenrick's waiting arms.

"I'm so excited, I couldn't sleep no matter how many times we made love," she said looking at her ring in the moonlight that beamed through the bedroom window of their thirty-fifth, top floor condo. She loved their room which was surrounded by floor to ceiling windows on all sides. Grabbing the remote, she opened the rest of the curtains to let more of the starry sky lit night in. Outside the window, she could see snow as it began to fall over the New York skyline.

"Is that so? Well, the night is still young and I may have a trick or two up my sleeve," Kenrick said nuzzling her neck and pulling her body close to his in the spooning position.

Justine held her hand out to allow them both to see it.

"This ring is beautiful. Someone may try to rob me to get this beauty off of my finger," she said.

"Not going to happen. There will be no Kim Kardashian moments in your future. That was a lesson learned for every celebrity. This ring is yours to wear whenever you want to and never if you don't. I have three other rings, much small, but just as special. You can interchange them up depending on what you're doing and where you're going. I would say if you're going to get your hair and nails done, you shouldn't wear it. If we're going to a star-studded event, yes, I want to see this rock on your finger. Of course, everything is insured, but more importantly, your life is the most important. You'll know what to do," Kenrick said.

"I love you so much," Justine whispered and leaned down to kiss the arm that Kenrick had wrapped around her body.

"That's why I love you. I've never known love like the love you brought into my life. You loved me unconditionally and that's what counted for me. I never thought I would have that or a family of my own and you gave me that. With you, Jazzy, Erick and Ricky, we arc as complete as a family could be. They bring so much of me out, love I never thought I could shower on another person. The four of you are my life. I'm glad you agreed to be my wife, something I should have done years ago, at least three kids ago," he joked.

Justine slapped him on the arm and then kissed where she'd just hit him.

"You got jokes, but I understand. Back then, you told me you wanted kids immediately and I could see how much it meant to you. I have always wanted kids, you know that so when you told me you were ready and I was ready, we had Ricky. The more kids we had, the more loving you became. All those bad memories from your childhood no longer have a place to call home. We're filling that space with the love of your own children and any more children we decide to have or adopt, whatever we decide to do. I know you have a passion for adopting and I want that, too. We have a lot of love to give."

Kenrick pulled her even closer to him.

"More love than I ever thought I would be able to give anyone."

Kenrick quickly recalled him telling her a few years back that it was his dream to adopt children who were left in the foster care system.

"Oh, congratulations on your win today. Things can only go up from here and these next few days, I can't wait to have fun as a family. We should probably get some sleep. Our little ones will be up pretty early looking for us. Hannah can get them breakfast, but they'll soon come rushing through our bedroom door ready to go out. It's getting late."

Kenrick looked at the clock on the nightstand.

"I forgot to make a phone call," he said.

"What call?" Justine asked as she watched him get out of bed and search for his phone.

"To the private investigator. He wanted to meet with Josiah and I tomorrow. I was supposed to call him tonight to set up a time tomorrow evening. He was planning to fly in from Los Angeles tomorrow morning."

"You're going to call him tonight?" she asked.

"It's two in the morning here, but it's only eleven in Los Angeles and he does his best work late at night. You go ahead and get some sleep and I'll step out into the living room to make this call so that I don't keep you up. I won't be long."

Kenrick slipped on some gym shorts and a t-shirt he found in his bag and left the bedroom, closing the door behind him as he made his call.

"Ivan," he said when the investigator answered the line. "I hope it's not too late to be calling," he added.

"No, not at all, Kenrick. Good game tonight. I think you're going all the way. How many rings will this be for you if you win?" Ivan asked.

"This will be number three," Kenrick exclaimed.

"I see it in your future. Now, I assume you're calling about our meeting? I'll be in New York tomorrow for another meeting and I was hoping you and Josiah had time to talk to me about some new information I have for you."

"We're ready to meet at whatever time you say. Is this anything you can share with me now?" Kenrick asked.

"Absolutely. Your sister is excited about meeting you and your brother. I didn't tell her who you were, but that you have the same father. She lives with her mother and stepfather and though her mother doesn't know who you are, she confirmed that Joseph Wilson was your sister's father. Her name is Bethany and she lives in North Carolina, where they moved to years ago. As I already shared with you, she is one year younger than you and when you see her, you'll think you're looking at the female version of yourself. She gets her skin tone and looks from the father you share. Her mother is open to her getting to know you, though Bethany is grown. She remembers how horrible your father was and wanted to be sure he wasn't in the picture before letting him loose on Bethany. I told her that your father had passed way and that's the only reason she gave her concurrence about the meeting. She didn't want your father anywhere near Bethany. I didn't tell her your name or anything else personal about you. I told her you were a nice person and that Bethany will enjoy getting to know her brothers."

Kenrick smiled. His family was getting larger and he loved it. He now had a brother and sister.

"What about the youngest two, the twins my father spoke of before he died."

Kenrick paced back and forth on the plush white carpet, excited that his efforts to surround himself with family was paying off.

"That's the biggest news I have for you. I found them. They are much younger than I thought they would be. They are twins and they're only ten years old. It looks like, even though your father was well into his forties, their mother was twenty-two at the time. She tried for a few years to care for them, but couldn't afford it after your father bailed on her. Her own parents had thrown her out and she lived from place to place with them until the state of New York finally took the kids away after she neglected them one time too many. They were five at the time and have lived in foster care ever since."

Kenrick couldn't breathe as he stopped moving. All

he could visualize was his siblings being mistreated like he had been as a child, first by his mother, then by his father and lastly by the foster family he had been placed with before he ran away and came to live with Paul and Minnie. The twins were his blood and he wanted them out of that environment, immediately.

"I want them out of foster care, Ivan. Are you sure they're my siblings?" he asked. Kenrick tried to shake off the uneasiness he felt knowing what could be happening to them.

"I'm one hundred percent sure. A blood test will be needed and you'll need to get a lawyer to petition the court to get them. Are you sure that's what you want if they turn out to be your brother and sister? That's a lot to take on. Didn't you tell me you have three kids of your own already?" Ivan asked.

"I do and yes I'm sure. They have family and don't need to be in foster care. I'll have my attorney come with us to the meeting tomorrow. I want the ball rolling immediately," he demanded. He took a deep breath as he tried to calm and control his anger.

Kenrick could feel his pressure rising as he paced around the living room. He knew he had more siblings, but had no idea they were that young. His father said they were young, but he wasn't sure he believed him.

"I hear you. I have a lot of pictures and paperwork with my notes for you to look over tomorrow when we meet. Again, like your sister, they look like mini versions of you. As soon as we petition the court, we can get the blood test and if things turn out, I don't see any reason why the court wouldn't award you custody. It doesn't happen overnight, so you'll have to be patient," Ivan said.

Kenrick didn't care anything about being patient. His years in foster care flashed across his eyes and though he knew it wasn't every kid's experience to go through what he did, he feared the worse.

"I'll talk with my wife and Josiah tomorrow morning. How is around three in the afternoon looking for you? I know Josiah is free and I'll call my attorney in the morning. With the retainer I pay him, he'll be available."

"Good. I'll see you tomorrow. Try to keep it together for now. This is moving along at a good pace and I want to be sure we're doing this all by the books."

Kenrick calmed his fast beating heart and knew Ivan spoke the truth. He had to let the process work itself out.

"I hear you and thanks for all you've done. I have one more question for you. What are their names?" he asked. He held his breath for what seemed an eternity before Ivan responded.

"Their names are Kelly and Kyle. Your father named them. I'll see you tomorrow," Ivan said.

"Yes, you will," Kenrick declared as he hung up.

He didn't go right back to the bedroom. Instead, he walked over to the large bay window and looked out over the New York sky. Somewhere out there in foster care, he had a little sister and brother whose names were Kelly and Kyle and they were ten years old. The only thing on his mind was getting them out of foster care. He would have some major decisions to make and he needed to talk it over with Justine. He wanted his brother and sister with him and that would mean two more children in their house. It would be a lot to take in and deal with, but he knew with love, all things were possible.

Letting go of the anxiety of the next steps, he walked back toward the bedrooms. He walked first into the boy's room to check on them and found them still sleeping soundly. After walking out and closing the door behind him, he went to look in on Jazzy. Expecting to find her asleep, he was surprised to see her wiggling around with her fingers in her mouth. The moment she saw him, she started to whine and reach for him. He needed to have her close to him tonight. Picking her up, he checked to see if she needed to be changed. Finding her dry, he put her laid her on his should where she gripped his neck with her little fingers. He walked into the bedroom where he found Justine asleep. Not wanting to wake her until Jazmine cried to be fed, he walked over to the love seat in the room and sat down with Jazmine in his lap. All he wanted to do was sit and reflect on how blessed his life was.

Epilogue
Six months later

Kenrick and Justine's house was buzzing with all kinds of activity. Hours earlier, they'd had their wedding ceremony on the lawn of their own house as they stood on the steps of the gazebo where they loved spending a lot of time together. Surrounding them in an atmosphere that had been constructed into a fairytale scene, family and friends stood as they declared their undying love for each other.

Now that the wedding was over, everyone dined and danced under the four tents that had been set up for celebration. Everyone had been asked to wear white for the day and the room had been decorated in their favorite colors of red and white.

Justine looked lovely in her Vera Wang gown, her second change of the night. Kenrick felt proud in his custom made white tuxedo. Their children stood with them, though it took a lot of wrangling to get Jazmine to stand still. She had recently learned to walk and loved how fast her little legs could carry her. She didn't like for anyone to tell her to be still.

Looking out from their view on the raised stage inside of the first tent, Kenrick smiled at his parents, Paul and Minnie and silently said thanks for all they had done to make him the man he was today. He waved at his sister, Andrea who flew in from Paris with her fiancé. He was happy to hear that they would be moving back to the United States to live. He loved that he would have her close again.

He rejoiced as he saw his brother dancing with his wife and having a good time. Sitting at a table right in front of his table was the sister he didn't know he had. Months ago, after Ivan connected them, they had been as close as some brothers and sisters who had lived their whole lives together. Ivan was right when he said looking at Bethany was like looking at the male version of himself. Now, that they were family, everyone they encountered asked if they were twins. They weren't, but they were family and that meant everything to him. Though Bethany lived in North Carolina, they talked several times a week and he was happy to hear she was a football fan.

What he was most proud to see was his little sister and brother, all decked out in their white dress and tuxedo. He was overwhelmed knowing that his family was complete for now.

After waiting for the blood test to confirm they were related, he had to go through the foster care process to get temporary custody of them. Once he got the news that they were his siblings, he jumped in his car and went to visit them. He was happy to know that they foster care home where they lived was a happy one. They were happy, loving and respectful kids and their foster parents opened their door to him to visit anytime until the situation was cleared up. He didn't gain custody right way and the moment he found out they were his sister and brother, he talked with Justine about his plan to bring them into their household and she didn't wait a breath before telling him she was all-in. Not surprising, he expected that reaction from her and like him, she wanted them out of foster care as soon as possible, not because they were being mistreated, but because they had a family who wanted to love and care for them.

Three months after everything had been confirmed and because of who he was, he was able to get his case expedited through the court system and Kelly and Kyle came to live with them in Alpine. Thankful for the great care their foster parents gave them, Kenrick made sure they would always be a part of Kelly and Kyle's life.

Transitioning the twins into their lives wasn't hard. He'd spent so much time with them that he fell in love with them instantly and they loved him, too. At first, the twins came for weekends to let their boys get used to having them around. When he explained who they were, Erick and Ricky took to them like they had known each other for years.

They redecorated the rooms so that Kyle could room with Erick and Ricky. Some people liked to separate their kids into their own rooms, by Kenrick wanted them to be each other's best friends.

They let Kelly have a hand in decorating her room the way she wanted and she and Justine bonded as if they were mother and daughter. Their favorite thing to do together was to go to the hair and nail salon.

Kenrick couldn't think of a more perfect life lived by anyone.

"Are you okay?" Justine asked, leaning over to him.

"I'm perfect. Look at this scene. Look at all of our family in one place celebrating together. This day is perfect," he said pulling her hands up to kiss the back of them.

"Thank you for being you," Justine said.

"Thank you for loving all of me, the good and the bad. My life is because of who you are. Look at Kelly and Kyle having a good time dancing. My sister Bethany is here and we're all together. We may have had a father that didn't care about us, but we're together despite that. This is all I've ever wanted in life. You, my kids and a family that I love and that love me."

"You got that baby. Thank you for taking that knee for our love," Justine said. "Let's dance."

More from Cheryl Barton

The Bachelor Series
Book 1 - Bachelor Not for Sale – Now available

Duron Knight agreed to take part in a bachelor auction held by his sister's sorority. Little did he know that he would find the woman of his dreams in the form of sexy bombshell Taija Charles, the woman in red.

Taija, in a room full of the sexiest men in Atlanta, has eyes for one handsome bachelor that no woman in her right mind could resist.

As sparks fly between them, can Duron put his unhappy past with women behind him and give his all to Taija? He may fight love, but Taija has plans to help him mend his broken heart with real love and a whole lot of lust.

Book 2 – A Designed Affair – Now available

In this follow-up to "Bachelor Not for Sale", Loren Knight has been engaging in a secret love affair with her brother Duron's best friend and business partner, Michael Bailey. He is everything she could want and more in a man, but she believes the risk is too great for any type of relationship with him beyond their steamy encounters behind closed doors.

Michael Bailey has been fighting his attraction to Loren for years. He has stayed away from her out of respect for his best friend and business partner. Now that he and Loren have finally given into the passion they have been craving, can Michael convince Loren that what they share is worth the risk of even Duron finding out?

Book 3 – *A Perfect Combination* – Now available

In this second follow-up to "Bachelor Not for Sale", Tyrone Davis is the king of one-night stands. The nickname, Mr. Love'em and Leave'em, given to him in his college days, still follows him as a top executive in the corporate world. He never believed in karma until it paid him a visit in the form of a very sexy and uninhibited one-night stand.

Victoria Alston couldn't forget the incredible night she spent with Tyrone Davis, someone connected to her best friends. In just one night, he stirred feelings in her she never thought she would ever experience. The next day, she disappeared, returning to reality and the fiancé she left back in Boston.

Tyrone and Victoria both soon discover that it wasn't just a one-night stand, but a perfect combination for the kind of love most people only dream about.

Book 4 – *Love at Last* – Now available

They had the perfect love...That's what Brian Knight thought of his relationship with Sherry Braxton until he looked up one day and she was gone and never wanted to see him again.

Two years later, he discovered that there is the possibility that Sherry may have been pregnant with his child. Hurt and angry at her deceit, he takes a flight to Baltimore to fight for his rights as a father and realizes that the love and passion they once shared had never died.

Is it possible he could still have the kind of love he thought would last a lifetime? Can he still have his love at last?

Enjoy this excerpt from "Snowbound", book 1 in the Second Chances series.

"She's divorcing me, Jay. Ten years of giving her everything and instead of being happy living this life of power, money and respect, she decides it's not enough for her; instead my marriage is about to be over."

Vincent Alonzo, entrepreneur and media mogul was venting to his best friend about his impending divorce from the woman he would move heaven and earth for. If anyone could help him get through this, he knew that Jay would. If no one was in his corner, he knew that he would always be able to look around and see his best friend, Jay Woodson having his back.

"I know Vin. You still haven't talked to her, huh?" Jay said, feeling his best friend's pain. When Vin hurt, he hurt. They had been best friends since high school and business partners since the beginning of their early rap careers. Together they'd turned their rap careers into business enterprises making them two of the richest men in the industry. It was apparent that even money couldn't buy them the happiness they wanted most, at least not for Vin. Jay was as happy in love as he could be and wished things hadn't turned out so bad for his friend.

"No, she won't talk to me. Her attorney told her to not discuss anything about the divorce without representation, as if I'd try and take advantage of her. I love her, man and I'm the last person that would do anything to hurt her or our children. They are my life and all I do, I do for them."

"Vin, we know that, but you know how these lawyers are. They see dollars signs, especially when it comes to being at the table opposite the powerful Vincent Alonzo. With the position you're in, you should know that. They aren't thinking about her, they're thinking about their own pay day."

"That may be the case, but Cara knows better. She knows me better than anyone, especially any lawyer. For a long time, we tried to meet and talk, but once we acquired the television network, time just got away from me and it never happened. The only time we really talked was about things that involved the kids. The few times I tried to ask her about it, were over the phone or in passing and she brushed me off saying any discussion about our marriage deserved more than a phone conversation or a conversation in passing. I can't believe that was a year ago. Now the time is here and I feel lost."

Vin paced back and forth wondering how he was going to live without Cara being his wife. She would forever be the mother of his children, but she was more than that and he needed her to be more than that. He needed her as his wife, the woman he loved with everything.

"Well from my vantage point, the fat lady hasn't sung yet and until you both sign on the dotted line, there's always time to work it out. Look, why don't you get out of here and get some space. I'll take care of the meetings today. You're not focused anyway."

Vincent was thankful that he had the kind of friendship with Jay that they'd developed over the years. The moment he walked into the office this morning, he was unfocused, though he knew he had several meetings to oversee. The moment he walked into Jay's office, that fact that he wasn't himself was the first thing Jay picked up on. His mind wasn't ready or anything business related.

He'd gotten up early, dressed in his favorite Calvin Klein suit knowing he still needed to keep up appearances around the office. The quietness of the condominium where he'd taken up residence after the separation from Cara seemed cold and lonely without the sound of his kids running around or of Cara telling him how handsome he looked. Where had time gone, he thought? Now, he was close to being a bachelor again and though some men love that life, he wasn't about it. He loved being married and he loved Cara. Jay was right, he needed some space.

"You're right. I can't remember the last time I've chilled at my condo. I'm usually rushing around to get out to one business thing or another or I'm in there asleep from exhaustion. I still have boxes I haven't unpacked yet. I'm headed there if you need me," Vin said, giving his partner a few more details on the day's meetings before getting some space between him and the multi-million-dollar company he'd built from nothing. Right now, it actually felt like nothing because even though he should be sitting on top of the world because he was literally sitting on top of the world, it meant nothing knowing Cara, the love of his life would no longer be at his side. He couldn't believe she was okay with them just existing in each other's lives.

Stopping by his office on his way out, he gave his two assistants, Marci and Natalie, instructions on what they should focus on and that in an emergency situation, they could find him at home.

He grabbed several files he wanted to look over, but had plans to focus on nothing work related if he could make it happen. While business was booming, his personal life was tanking and for the first time in his life, he felt like he had no control.

Standing in his office looking around, Vin made sure he took a mental check of everything he would need, placed items in his briefcase and closed his office door. His assistants would make sure everyone knew he wasn't in for the day and that there would be no need for anyone to enter his office.

"Mr. Alonzo, are there any calls in particular that you want me to forward to you or none at all?"

Vincent walked up to Marci and saw the bewildered look on her face. When he glanced over at Natalie, he saw the same look. He knew that they were wondering what was going on with his odd behavior. He never came in the office and then left right after with instructions that he should not be contacted. Usually his instruction was to forward calls to his phone and send him any emails that were important. Today, he didn't want any of that. His personal life was tanking and he needed to figure a way to get a grip on what the norm was about to be for him.

"No calls, no emails. Anything important, send to Mr. Woodson's office, otherwise, we can touch base when I return."

"Will that be tomorrow?" Marci asked.

"Possibly. I will call you first thing in the morning if I'm taking extra time. I know this is out of the ordinary for me, but these are not ordinary times for me. Mr. Woodson and other members of leadership are around if you need something. Of course, I'm always available to both of you if you have a need that only I can deal with. In that case, call me on my cell. That good?" he asked.

When Marci and Natalie smiled, he felt better about leaving them in a lurch, something he never does.

"Yes," they said together.

Vince nodded and walked toward the elevator. He nodded at people he encountered or those who spoke to him, but he avoided lingering eye contact to alleviate any need for a long conversation. Now that he was leaving, he was anxious to get out of the building. Luckily, he entered the elevator alone and it went straight to the garage without stopping. Thankfully, his driver hadn't gotten too far away after dropping him off that he could turn around and come back to the garage to pick him up. As soon as he'd left Jay's office, he sent Darren a text that if he was still close by, he needed a ride back to his condo. Darren, being the dedicated staffer, replied he was on his way back and headed for the garage.

Getting in the back of the truck, Vince thanked him for being conscientious and then after a few moments of chatter, his thoughts turned to Cara. He couldn't describe in words how much he missed going to bed and waking up to her. Needing to hear her voice, he asked Darren to raise the dividing glass giving him some privacy. He needed to try and talk to Cara again. As usual he got her voicemail. He had no problem leaving another message and hoped that she was at least listening to them.

"Cara it's me. I wish you would talk to me. Things are getting serious now and it's crazy that we can't even have a conversation. This divorce is no joke. Is this really what you want? You could at least talk to me. You really want to leave me? Why are we letting a lawyer dictate when we can and cannot talk about this? I admit I haven't made myself the most available the times you wanted to talk, but I'm willing to talk now, so just call me back, please. Kiss the kids for me and tell them I'll see them for my weekend. I don't know how some parents do this for years on end. I miss them and I miss you even though you're divorcing me. I hope we get to talk before that happens. Let me know and I can have a car pick you up and bring you to *Shatori's* for dinner. Call me," he said and hung up.

Turning to look out of the truck window as they whizzed through traffic, he hoped he sounded as defeated as he felt. He wanted her to know what this divorce was doing to him. He knew it would be only a matter of days now before it would be over and like Jay said, until the fat lady sings, he was determined to get to the bottom of the reason behind the divorce. Cara claiming irreconcilable differences meant nothing to him. He wanted to know exactly what the problems were and maybe he could fix them. Things had gotten to a point that she didn't want to talk about anything anymore. He moved out because of her wishes and their issues and lack of communicating was beginning to have an impact on their kids. He may have done it, but he wasn't happy.

Enjoy chapter 1 of "Love on Top", a new release by Cheryl Barton

The minute Dakota heard the phone ringing throughout the house and she knew it was already pretty late in the evening, the only person calling this late had to be Brandon calling with another story or excuse to try and explain another late, late night working. Despite how relaxing her day had been, she could feel frustration creeping up her spine. Her first inkling was to let it ring and not answer, but she knew if it was him, he'd get anxious knowing she was at home with their kids alone. After getting no response, knowing Brandon the way she did, he would continue calling between the house phone and her cell phone until he got an answer and if still nothing, he'd come flying through the door, worried at first and then angry that she'd made him terrified with thoughts that something bad could have happened to them. Maybe he needed to worry more if that meant he'd come home. Despite how angry she was at his increasing number of extended absences lately, she didn't want to put him through the unnecessary angst that something could be wrong at home.

With as much attitude as she could muster up, she snatched up the house phone from the nightstand before it stopped ringing.

"What is it this time, Brandon?" she said before giving him a chance to say hello. The patience she typically tried to maintain when it came to him had flown out the door weeks ago when the excuses for his absence around the house started to become the norm.

When she married him eight years ago, a year after graduating from college, she never expected to get to a day when she'd start feeling like a single parent raising their children by herself. Even the kids started noticing his absence and were asking for him more than they ever have before. Each time she made up an excuse for him not being around, she saw the look of disappointment on their faces. She could handle being disappointed by Brandon, though it still bothered her, but she wasn't going to continue to accept what it was doing to their children. Jasmine at seven and Braden at four should expect to have both of their parents actively involved in their lives on a daily basis.

"I can't get a hello before you give me attitude and go nuclear?" Brandon asked.

It didn't escape her that he was trying to keep the mood light knowing that unless he was calling to say he was on his way, the conversation wasn't going to go well.

"When you're calling this late at night for the fourth time this week and we're only five days in and I suspect I know the reason for this call, I'm not in the mood for dishing out hellos. I assume this is another call about something important or some emergency again at the club or at the construction site and I shouldn't expect you anytime soon. Am I in the ballpark?" she asked with enough irritation in her voice to make sure her frustration with him was crystal clear.

Hearing Brandon huff on the other end of the phone angered her more. What did he have to be upset about? He was living the life having his home life taken care of and in perfect condition whenever he decided to come home and spend time with his wife and children. If she didn't know any better, she'd think that he was cheating on her. All the signs were there – his being gone all the time, especially after hours, his disinterest in anything family related and their lack of intimacy over the past few months. Brandon's appetite for sex was voracious and had been since the first time they'd made love when they were in college. She loved how even after years of marriage, he couldn't seem to get enough of her, until lately that is, but something in their love life had changed and she was worried.

"You know what I'm trying to do and it's all about business, so I don't get why I receive disdain and anger from you. Everything I do, I do for you and the kids and you know that. Without everything I'm doing, we wouldn't have the life we're living, so a little more support from you would be appreciated," he said curtly.

Hearing his tone, the conversation was headed down the same path that it always seemed to go and it wasn't a happy one.

Dakota had to hold the phone out and look it over to be sure she heard what she thought she heard. For an instant, she had a premise that her husband had lost his mind. She was nothing but supportive and had been since the day they'd met. She was the dutiful wife maintaining the home, taking care of the kids and helping out with his businesses whenever he needed her. What she didn't support or sign up for was a husband who spent more time away from home than in it. She wanted more of Brandon, more of the man she married eight years ago who made her a priority in his life. She no longer felt like she was in that position and it bothered her.

"Don't talk to me like I don't support you every day with everything you do. I am your biggest supporter despite the fact that I see less and less of you with every passing day. I deserve just as much time as your business ventures. As soon as I think it's getting better and you've reached an achievement, you start something new and you're away more and more. I thought tonight we were going to have a family night and the kids were looking forward to it. Every time lights passed down our street, they would look toward the garage to see if they could hear you pulling in. We don't usually get a lot of traffic because there are only four houses in our secluded development, but it seemed like a major highway of traffic tonight, the one night they were really looking forward to time alone with you. When they finally fell asleep in the family room, I put them to bed and knew that I shouldn't even think about waiting up for you. If you're calling about another late night, save it. I guess there's no need in waiting up."

"Dakota, aren't you tired of fighting with me all the time about the same thing? I'm sorry about tonight, but it couldn't be avoided."

"Of course not. I have no doubt it couldn't be avoided because nothing around here is as much a priority as your latest money-making endeavor, right?"

Dakota sat up in bed, bracing for an intense discussion because there was no way she was going to let him sugarcoat his lack of time and attention to his family.

"That's not fair and you know it," he said.

"Really? Not fair? What is really going on, Brandon? Is it really work that's taking up your time or something else? Is it another woman? Women? All these late nights, it can't always be work. You're gone all day starting the moment the sun comes up and then all evening and well into the night. You come home long enough to change and remind us that you are still a part of this family and then you're gone again. You make plans with me and the kids and then you cancel with one excuse after another. What happened to the family trip we were going to take before the kids start school in a few weeks? They only have a little over a month left before the first day of school and we had planned to take them to Disney World, to the beach, to other amusement parks and instead, I end up taking them someplace to make up for the fact that you've found something more important to you than your family," she pleaded with exasperation.

"It's midnight, Dakota and I don't want to get into this with you again and again. I don't have to call and tell you I'm going to be late like I have to check-in; I'm doing it because it's the right thing to do, but if you're going to get all crazy about it every time, then I won't do it at all," he countered angrily.

"Seriously, if you think you're doing me a favor by calling me late night to say you'll be home sometime before the sun comes up, save yourself the breath. I preferred the days of the past when you would call this late at night for a booty call, but I guess getting married and having kids, you no longer feel that's a necessity, you know, that thing called paying attention to your wife. Hey, you consider it an imposition to do anything but work these days, so you do that. I've had enough excuses to last me a lifetime."

"Well, I miss having a wife who understands the importance of what I'm doing. Where is that woman?"

Dakota's anger now boiled over.

"You know where she is? She's at home in bed alone for another night wondering if her husband has found another bed to warm at night because it's clear it's not the one at the house where he lives. She's here taking care of your house and your children, making sure that despite having an absentee father, they are still happy and thriving. She's here being everything you need when you need it and she has a right to question when providing needs is no longer a two-way street. You know what? I am tired of fighting Brandon, so screw you and good night."

Before he could respond, Dakota hung up and then unplugged the phone. She didn't even want to be tempted to answer if he called back.

After turning out the light on the nightstand, she

rolled over and tried to focus on anything that would help her fall asleep since she was amped up after another nasty fight.

Her mind took her back to happier times before and right after they married.

She'd met Brandon through his sister, Alisha, who she had been best friends with since their freshman year in college at Norfolk State in Virginia. Brandon, their brother Aiden and their parents had come to the school to support Alisha for her first time on the field as a dancing majorette. After the game, Alisha introduced her to the family and there were sparks between her and Brandon that couldn't be denied. From that day, they were inseparable. Brandon and Aiden, who were twins, were juniors in college at Howard University and as often as he could get away, he would drive down to Norfolk on weekends and they would hang out. Those weekends helped make her first time being away from home enjoyable.

Brandon was unlike most of the guys she knew back at home in Philadelphia where she had been born and raised. Most didn't have dreams beyond getting out of high school, but Brandon knew he was going to make something big out of life and he was making plans to achieve that even while still in school. She loved that his plans included big dreams with major successes and also included a life with her.

In her sophomore year, her father was able to buy her a used car and once she and Alisha were on the road, all of their spare time was spent between Howard and Norfolk and they ended up being more like sisters than just college roommates. They not only took road trips to Howard University, but they would drive to Baltimore where Alisha was from and she'd show her around town.

After graduating college, with Brandon and Aiden already using their degrees in Business Management and opening up their first night club together, Dakota was surprised when Brandon proposed to her in front of her family at her college graduation party. His family was also in attendance and other than the day they'd met, it was the happiest day of her life. From there, life was a big rollercoaster ride. She'd planned their wedding which was the kind little girls dreamed about. A year later, they welcomed their first child and she'd never looked back until lately.

She and Brandon agreed early that as long as they could afford it, she would stay home until the kids were old enough to be in school all day. She didn't mind because she loved bonding and spending time with the kids, time she'd never get back if they were in daycare all day while she worked. Her degree in Accounting could take her in many directions eventually and she didn't have a problem waiting until her kids were older to dive into the working world.

Brandon provided a great life for them. After their wedding, she moved to Miami where he and Aiden had moved to open their first club. That club instantly became the hottest spot in the Miami Beach area, a favorite of celebrities around the world. With the success of that club, they opened up several supper clubs and three other popular restaurants and bars inside of three five-star hotels.

Business was booming, but in the midst of all of that success, their home life began to suffer, especially when they decided to open a second location for their nightclub. Due to the popularity of the first one, they often maxed out on the number of patrons early in the night and knew it was time to expand. That expansion had led to long days and nights of Brandon being away from her and the children.

By now, she thought life would be different and once Brandon and Aiden were successful, they would hire the people they needed to run their businesses and she would get her husband back, giving them more family time before the kids got too big to appreciate having experiences of vacations that some kids never get to experience. Most didn't because of a lack of money, but she never imagined her kids wouldn't because of the lack of a parent being around.

Dakota tossed around on the bed and turned back to face her nightstand where a picture of her and Brandon sat. It was a picture taken on the island of Jamaica where they went for their honeymoon and it was where they made commitments to each other to always place family first and to always put their love first. She'd done everything to make that happen and yet she felt like their love was slipping away.

She tried going to where he was in order to spend time with him, but times where she would go to the club, Brandon was so busy running things that he didn't have time to have a drink or even dance with her. She understood he had a business to run, but there were times when that was the only time that she got to see him. She hated thinking of the conversations she'd overhear of women talking about him and all the things they like to do to him. She'd watch them flaunt shamelessly in front of him and he appeared to be sucking up all that attention. He told her that it was all a part of the business and it's only successful if people enjoyed being in the club. Still, knowing the things these women were willing to do just to get closer to him, she wondered how much declining a man could actually do before he indulged, especially when his wife and children were safely tucked away at home.

After having two children, she wasn't sure she was still as sexy to him as some of the young hot women in little black dresses he encountered nightly and those type of thoughts began to play havoc with her mind. Nothing she did seemed to interest him or perhaps, as Alisha said to her, it was all in her mind.

During one of their outings, she'd told Alisha about her reservations about pending problems in her marriage and Alisha brushed it off and told her that Brandon had loved her since the first moment she'd introduced them and that she had nothing to worry about. Still, something was wrong and she didn't know how to fix it. They were growing apart and she didn't know how to bridge the gap.

Thinking of what could be happening to her

marriage caused her eyes to mist over and a tear fell down her cheek and onto the pillow. As she laid in bed alone, something she has been doing a lot of lately, her mind couldn't help, but wander to the possibility that Brandon had tired of her and had moved on to someone else, someone younger, sexier, hotter and not married to him. That caused her to cry even harder until sleep took over.

About the Author

Cheryl Barton lives in Maryland and in her spare time she loves to read espionage novels, cook, watch Sci-fi movies, spend time with family and friends and enjoy Maryland steamed crabs.

Indulge in more romance and inspirational novels by visiting her website at www.cherylbarton.net.

Cheryl is a member of the Romance Writers of America – National Chapter and the Maryland Romance Writers.

Connect with the Author

Website www.CherylBarton.net or
www.crbarton.com
Twitter – @Author Cheryl Barton
Instagram – AuthorCherylBarton
Facebook at Author Cheryl Barton
Email – Cheryl@CherylBarton.net
Blog - https://mswriterinmd.wordpress.com/

www.ingramcontent.com/pod-product-compliance
Lightning Source LLC
Chambersburg PA
CBHW050819180626
46814CB00004B/1368